# SHE WHO HAS A MAN ...

A novel

*And they were both naked, the man and his wife, and were not ashamed.*

*Genesis 2:25 NKJV*

# Taiwo Iredele Odubiyi

Copyright May 2022 by Taiwo Iredele Odubiyi

ISBN: 9798358830790

Published by:
Tender Heartslink,
Maryland, USA.

WhatsApp: +1(443)694-6228
Website: www.pastortaiwoodubiyi.org
Facebook: Pastor (Mrs.) Taiwo Odubiyi,
    Pastor Taiwo Iredele Odubiyi's Novels & Books,
    Tenderheartslink with Pastor Taiwo Odubiyi
Twitter: @pastortaiwoodub

Instagram: @pastortaiwoiredeleodubiyi

This is a work of fiction. The characters, incidents, and dialogues are products of the author's imagination and are not to be construed as real. Any resemblance to actual events or persons, living or dead, is entirely coincidental.

All rights reserved. No part of this publication may be reproduced or transmitted in any form or by any means—electronic, mechanical, photocopying, recording, publishing, film production, or any other—without the prior written permission of the copyright holder.

# PRAISE FOR THE BOOKS
## OF TAIWO IREDELE ODUBIYI

*A Christmas to Remember* - Absolutely, a beautiful story. Really inspiring, thought provoking, romantic. Hmm. Really, excellent, a blessing! Most importantly bringing the word of God to shed light on this issue of divorce which unfortunately has almost become a menace in the church. It is 'packed.' Thanks for writing!! - *Lenient Bilewu (Mrs.) USA*

I've been blessed by your books. I came across your books when I was way back in secondary school—seventeen (17) years ago—and I was absolutely blessed. I read *Love on the Pulpit* and this helped me to once again have a resolute to keep myself for my husband. To the glory of God, I'm happily married to a man of God and that resolution the Lord helped me keep – *Ateji Damilola, Nigeria*

Ever since 2012 when I read my first Pastor Taiwo Iredele Odubiyi book, I made myself a promise to be a collector of her books ... not just for me but for my kids in the nearest future. I just had this knowing that life then would be different. A decade after, I have more than fifteen of her books and recently got three new ones. I love the legacy that I'm building... – *Toluwakemi, Abeokuta, Nigeria*

I just bought six of your books last week. During a Sunday school review in my church some months ago, we gave out your amazing books to our Sunday school students 😊 – *Aramide Oluwa, Alagbado, Nigeria*

Good morning, Ma 😊. I would like to share my experience with you. I came across your books in Bible Wonderland yesterday. I went to Bible Wonderland with my younger sister and searched in vain for our usual Christian fiction. My sister stumbled on the isle your books were and sceptically we bought *I'll take you there.* Immediately we got home, we started reading and I was so blessed 💯. The story line wasn't cliché, it had a strong message. The description was sooo accurate and the blend of Yoruba and English was top notch. I immediately fell in love with your books and I plan to purchase many in the future. Thank you for being a force to reckon with in the Christian romance industry. God bless you, Ma - *Temitayo Omisope, Lagos, Nigeria*

I got to know your work of art through a neighbor from whom I collected *Love on the Pulpit*. Since then, I have been addicted to your books. I have bought and read up to fourteen of your books which have been a blessing to me and many people around me because I share the books with people around me, especially the married, and single men and women ... Keep up the good work. More anointing - *Temidayo Kayode-Akinyemi, Sagamu, Nigeria*

I got introduced to your novels through one of my friends while I was in secondary school and since then I have been hooked. When I haven't read the latest book, I go through withdrawal symptoms. Your books are so unique in the sense that as you are reading about godly relationship, you are also learning about fashion and cooking. May your oil never run dry. Thank you for yielding yourself to God. Happy 20th anniversary of writing for God – *Okunade Dorcas Olorunfemi, student, Akure, Nigeria*

Got my copy of *Accidentally Yours* and *Jonah's First Day of School*, last week. The book *Accidentally Yours* has been a lot of blessing to me. Have learnt a lot from all your books. I got all your books. Even some of them are two copies – *Monsurat Omidiran, Lagos, Nigeria*

*Accidental Yours* – I got mine this afternoon, I didn't drop it until I finished reading it. As usual, you got me captivated – *Adereti Esther OreOluwa*

I read this book already *Accidentally Yours,* and I was greatly blessed by it – *Boge A. AnuOluwapo, Ikorodu, Nigeria*

You're doing a great job. Just finished reading *Sea of Regrets* and *You Found Me*. Blessed as always – *Obakhena Joy, Lagos, Nigeria*

I just finished reading one of your novels *Shadows from the Past,* and I must say I am truly blessed. I will like to have more copies – *Victoria Opemipo*

I love this book, *Life Goes On*. I keep reading again and again – *Bamimosu Oluwatofarasin Mariam, Nigeria*

God bless you; you are indeed a great blessing to this generation and generations to come ... I have read almost all your books and I'm greatly blessed by them. Kudos to my class teacher who introduced me to your books – *Olukunle Peter, Ogbomoso, Nigeria*

May the Lord bless you, Pastor Taiwo for all these powerful novels. I can totally relate to Victor in *If You Could See Me Now* ... proudly PK – *Ajileye Motunrayo Adeosun*

I love this book *If You Could See Me Now*. I can read it a million times. Thank you so much for using your books to bless lives. The way you make it so real is amazing. Proudly a PK – *Ozenua Joy*

# EXCERPTS

... "And with a demanding job thrown into the mix, I just didn't have much time to give marriage a very serious thought."

"You didn't have much time to give marriage a very serious thought? Are you kidding me?"

Tokunbo laughed.

"I'll tell you what I think." Ruth said. "I guess it's because you haven't fallen in love with any of the sisters in your church. Because if you had, busy or not, the case would have been different and you'd be married by now."
...


... And when she was still thinking of him on Friday evening, a week later, she wondered what was happening. She had prayed to have a man like him, not him in particular! So where was this feeling coming from? ...


... Afterward, still wrapped in each other's arms, he looked at her lovingly and said, "I enjoyed that. What about you? Did you?"

Ruth smiled and nodded, her heart full of so much love and gratitude. "Umm hmm."

"What does that mean?" ...

# ACKNOWLEDGMENTS

I thank You, Lord God, the I AM, my Rescuer and Lord, For:

Yet another book. *Thank You for the great privilege and grace that You have given me to speak and write for You, and about You; about Your will, Your ways, Your word, and Your wondrous love. Thank You for the mercy You have shown me to know You;*

My husband and children- *for all that they do for me.*

All the wonderful family members You have blessed me with - *for always being there for me.*

TanitOluwa Odubiyi—my editor—*thank you for choosing to work with me. I appreciate you.*

Families, friends, and fans, my avid readers - those who have been with me since the beginning of this great journey, and those who joined along the way, reading my books, supporting, praying, and encouraging me.

Lord, let those who read this book be blessed, touched and transformed by You, that they may know that You are the real Author and Your mercy endures forever!

**It's All About You!**        **Taiwo Iredele Odubiyi**

# DEDICATION

To God

*For God so loved the world that He gave His only begotten Son, that whoever believes in Him should not perish but have everlasting life. (John 3:16 NKJV)*

She Who Has a Man | Taiwo Iredele Odubiyi

# CHAPTER 1

"Hi, good to see you again! Please come in." Ruth told her visitor, Desmond. Opening the door wider, she moved back to allow the man to come in.

Thirty-year-old Ruth who wore a loose man's shirt on loose fit jeans was a university graduate. Although she studied Economics, she learned photography while in school and was now a professional photographer.

"Thank you." Desmond responded and stepped inside the apartment. The dark-complexioned man was just coming from a construction site where he worked as an Engineer. The blue cotton shirt that he wore on jeans was slightly dirty on a side.

The time was seven-ten that Monday evening.

"How have you been?" Desmond asked Ruth.

"I've been good." She answered, smiling broadly. Ruth who wore glasses was slightly light-skinned, and slim. "And you?"

"Great!"

As Ruth closed the front door, one of the doors in the two-bedroom apartment opened and a lady came out.

Ruth turned around and still smiling broadly, she told Desmond, "This is Linda, my girlfriend." And looking at Linda, she pointed at the visitor and said, "This is Desmond."

"Hi." Linda greeted Desmond. Slim and dark in complexion, she wore a sleeveless top on ripped jeans shorts, and had long wavy hair.

"It's nice to meet you, Linda." Desmond said.

"Nice to meet you too."

As he shook hands with her, he looked her over. He didn't think she could be more than twenty six years.

"Please have your seat." Ruth told Desmond.

"Thank you." He said and sat down.

Linda opened another door and went inside.

"What do we offer you? We have beer, wine, soft drink-" Ruth asked Desmond.

"Any soft drink would be fine."

"Coca Cola?" Ruth wanted to know.

"Perfect."

"Alright, make yourself comfortable. I'll be right back." Ruth told him.

Ruth and Desmond attended the same University. During her first year in the University while he was in his second year, he had shown interest in her. However, when she turned him down and he insisted on knowing why she didn't want to be with him, she had to reveal to him that she was attracted to only her gender—she was a lesbian.

They remained friends but after his graduation, they lost touch until he contacted her yesterday. He'd found her page on Instagram—*Ruthy Photos*—and sent a message asking her to contact him. She'd called the phone number that he included in the message and they'd talked. He said he'd be getting married this year and when he asked if she'd be available to cover the event, she'd said yes but that they would need to talk further.

He'd also wanted to know if she was married and she'd said no. When she revealed that she had a girlfriend she lived with, he'd been surprised, and had asked her to send her house address to him so he could stop by on his way back from work to meet her girlfriend.

Now, as Ruth walked toward the kitchen, Desmond looked at her. With her very short hair, the clothes she wore, and the way she walked, it was obvious to him that she was the male figure in the lesbian relationship. She had not been this obvious in university though, he thought.

Desmond glanced around the living room. Beautiful framed photographs lined two sides of the room's white wall. Another side had a backdrop while the remaining wall was left plain. There were nice looking sofas, armchairs, high chairs, side tables, an area rug, lamps, mirrors, and light stands. The arrangement of the furniture made him believe that the room was used as a studio to take nice photographs. In a corner was a table on which were a laptop, printer, camera, and a cardholder, among other things. Ruth was doing well, Desmond concluded.

Just as Ruth was returning to the living room with a tray that contained a glass cup and bottle of Coca Cola, Linda emerged.

"You have a nice place here." Desmond said, and looked from Ruth to Linda.

"Thank you." Ruth responded and glanced around the room.

She had rented the place about a year ago, and it was one of the two apartments in a building that was at the back of a bungalow. The house owner lived in the bungalow with his family and rented out the two apartments in the back building. The back building had its own gate which meant that the occupants of the two apartments did not need to use the main gate that was in front of the bungalow. This was perfect for Ruth as her apartment doubled as her photo studio. Her friends, clients, and Linda could come and go through the back door without the whole house being in her business and gossiping about her.

Ruth was the third child in a family of four children, and her older brother and sister were married. Her younger sister, Rachel, was still single and lived with their parents.

None of her family members suspected anything about her sexuality when she was younger. Whenever her siblings discussed relationship and marriage, and asked her if she was seeing any man, she told them she was not ready for a relationship and they believed her. She had almost revealed the truth to her siblings several times, but somehow, she knew they would not understand or accept her preference. They would want her to marry a man but that was not for her.

And so, Ruth had been able to—with much struggle—hide her sexual preference from her family until the day her mother visited her on campus, unannounced, and found her in bed, passionately kissing a girl. Ruth was in her second year in the university.

"Mom!" She had said in surprise, and watched as her mother's face turned to stone.

The other lady jumped up from the bed and hurriedly adjusted her clothes. Taking her wallet, she wore her shoes, and left the room.

In shock, Ruth's mother had called her father on phone to report her, and her father had asked her to come home to see him the next day, unfailingly. Her mother shouted at her, cried, and eventually left. Shortly after, Ruth received calls from her siblings which she refused to answer. How she lived was her business, she decided.

At home the next day, she said as much to her parents and siblings who had been summoned by her mother. While her mother cried and her siblings looked at her in shock, her father—a bank manager—made her know that he would no longer pay her school fees until she changed.

Well, she was not ready to give up her lifestyle and change. There was nothing wrong with how she lived, Ruth said. *I know what's best for me.* She needed to be herself, and this was who she was. She convinced herself and hardened her heart.

Back on campus, she became a little more open about who she was. She also began to think of the kind of business she could do to make money and sustain herself. That was when one of her friends told her about photography. Initially, she was not interested but later changed her mind. She raised some money, learned photography, bought a camera and some necessities, and began the business right there on campus. Some of the students were aware of her sexual preference but didn't care much and patronized her. She was happy. There were some challenges, but she managed to cope.

Soon, some of her cousins and other family members heard about her lifestyle, but she was not bothered. She simply stayed away from those who were opposed to her decision—she was not going to allow them dictate to her.

She had been living at home with her parents and Rachel whenever the school was on break. However, after her graduation and NYSC (which was a year's mandatory national service by Nigerian University graduates), she moved out to stay with a friend. She moved twice after that, saved money, and eventually rented this two-bedroom apartment where she lived with Linda.

Ruth was five years older than Linda. They met eighteen months ago at a party and clicked right away. While people at the party danced and had fun, Ruth and Linda sat on a side and talked, to know each other better.

Linda told Ruth that she was two years old when her mother died. Then she was raised by her father and her only sibling sister who was eight years older than her. Linda had plans to go to university, and she already got admitted to one but the sudden death of her father put an end to her plans. Linda's married sister did not have a good job and couldn't afford to support her. Linda got herself a boyfriend to live with, and he gave her some money with which she enrolled in a catering school, and had a diploma. The boyfriend abused her however, and treated her like trash.

Linda would have left him, but thinking that she didn't have a choice, she stayed and endured the life of abuse. But the man eventually kicked her out, and she had to stay with a friend.

Shortly after, she met a well-paid movie actress who wanted to be with her. A man or a woman, Linda didn't care; what she cared about was money, love, and stability. She jumped at the opportunity that the much older actress offered her, especially since the actress promised to get her some acting roles. The actress fulfilled her promises, took care of Linda and gave her a role in a movie, but soon abandoned her for another willing female partner.

"I want commitment and stability. I want someone who will stay with me, and will not disappoint me." Linda had told Ruth at the party.

Looking into Linda's eyes, Ruth said, "You have found the person. Like you, I want commitment and stability. My previous girlfriends cheated on me ... and I think I've had enough of that."

"I won't cheat on you."

*Good.* "I will not leave you." Ruth promised.

Ruth had told Linda that she didn't like to cook, although she could hold her own in the kitchen, and Linda had assured Ruth not to worry about it. Aside from being a professional caterer, Linda loved to cook.

Ruth also made her know that she was staying with a friend, but she had enough money saved to rent an apartment. That was how she rented this apartment and Linda moved in with her. They shared the master bedroom which was bigger than the second bedroom and had an adjoining toilet and bath. The second bedroom, which served as a guest room, studio, and changing room for Ruth's clients, had a bed, closet, mirror, table, and a chair. The apartment had a visitor's toilet and bath, a big kitchen, and a balcony.

Linda had told her sister that Ruth was a friend with whom she shared an apartment and her sister believed her. The woman and her husband did not suspect that Linda was involved with Ruth especially since Linda had boyfriends in the past and looked every inch feminine—beautiful and fashionable with long hair.

When Linda explained to Ruth that she would have to lie to her sister about their relationship, Ruth understood and played along whenever the woman and her family visited. However, Ruth hoped that Linda would reveal the truth to them soon so she could stop pretending around them. The pretence was becoming more and more difficult for her.

Ruth's parents and siblings still talked to Ruth but none of them had come to the apartment since she got it. If her parents needed to see her, they asked her to come to their house while her siblings asked her to meet them at their parents' house or some other convenient place. Ruth could understand her parents' attitude, but couldn't understand why her siblings—especially the older ones—did not show more understanding, after all, she accepted them and their decisions. The lack of visit did not matter much to her though, as she was a reserved person who enjoyed her own company.

As if that was not enough, her younger sister, Rachel, suddenly became a Christian about five years ago in her final year in university. That was another thing that Ruth could not understand. None of the family members was serious about church, so why would Rachel decide to become 'born again'? *Whatever the phrase meant*! *What was wrong with her*? Well, that was Rachel's business; it was her life and she could do whatever she wanted with it but she should not try to preach to her, Ruth had decided. The few times Rachel tried to talk to her about Jesus, she had stopped Rachel with a warning. Having someone preach to her made her angry. And somehow afraid ...

... Ruth brought her mind back to the present and looked at Linda who was walking in the direction of their bedroom. She called Linda and said, "Desmond and I were in University together."

Linda stopped walking and turned to Ruth. "Oh, I see."

"He's getting married soon." Ruth added and put the tray on the side table near Desmond.

"Great!" Linda said and looked at Desmond, "Congratulations."

"Thank you." Desmond responded.

"He wants me to be the official wedding photographer." Ruth went on.

"Wise choice!" Linda said and sat on a sofa. "Ruth is very good; she will capture the day for you. She's one of the best choices in this part of the city."

"Well, that is if I can afford her." Desmond said and chuckled.

Ruth laughed. "Why not? My service is affordable."

"It is." Linda confirmed. "Besides, she's very good. Getting good pictures of your wedding is important, it's your big moment. Whatever amount you have to spend will be money spent wisely. You will definitely get good value for your money."

Desmond nodded. "I know. I saw some gorgeous images on her Instagram page and they are very beautiful. Even back in school, she was good."

"Thank you." Ruth said.

Ruth walked over, sat beside Linda, and taking her hand, she told Desmond, "Before we go on, Linda is into cakes, and she makes beautiful wedding cakes. If you don't have someone for your wedding cake yet, could you consider her?"

"Oh, someone's handling that already, but if I have her business card, I could tell some of my friends about her." Desmond replied.

"I'd appreciate that." Linda responded.

Ruth got up, walked over to the table where the laptop was, and took their business cards from the cardholder which she gave to Desmond. "These are our cards."

Returning to sit beside Linda, she asked Desmond, "So, when is the wedding?"

"It's still some time away. It's on December 19."

"December 19? Oh wow! That's eight months away!"

"Yes. My fiancé and I decided to start our wedding planning early so we can have plenty of time to get things done."

"That's right. Starting early is better, it makes sense." Ruth commented. "But is the date fixed? Are you sure it won't change?"

"No, it won't change. It's fixed." Desmond confirmed. "Even the wedding venue has been booked."

"Alright. The day should be free for me. I'll just check." Ruth said and then opened the planner on her phone. "Oh, great! I don't have anything slated for the day yet, so I'll just slot you in."

"Okay, but how much do you charge?" Desmond asked.

They discussed at length for about an hour, agreed on the price, and when Desmond eventually got up to leave, Linda said goodbye, while Ruth got up to see him off.

As soon as the door closed behind them, Desmond said, "Wow! You seem to be doing well."

Ruth laughed. "Thank you."

"And you and Linda seem to love each other."

"Yes, we do." She said proudly with a nod.

"You seem happy." Desmond added.

"I am." Ruth confirmed with a nod. She was happy with her life. She was a good photographer and more jobs were coming in. She also had a girlfriend, a car, and accommodation. She had about all that she wanted, she guessed. And like an icing on cake, she was not under the control of anyone. She was in control of her life. She was her own boss.

"For how long have you and Linda been together?" Desmond wanted to know.

Smiling, Ruth answered, "About a year and a half."

"How old is she?"

"She's twenty five."

"Wow! How is your family taking this?" He asked. "I'm sorry if I seem to be asking too many questions."

"It's okay, feel free to ask me any question." Ruth said, still smiling. She did not mind his questions. As a matter of fact, she preferred being asked questions than to be ignored or given a bad look as some people did.

"So, is your family okay with this?" Desmond went on.

"Not really, but I don't care much about their opinion. I don't give a flip what they think. I'm an adult and it's my life." She said nonchalantly.

"I'm just wondering."

Ruth nodded. "I know."

Desmond smiled. "My own parents would have killed me if I did that—that is if the news did not kill them first."

Ruth shrugged. "Well, it is what it is."

Desmond spoke again, "Do you and Linda intend to make things official at some point or how does this relationship work? I'm curious."

"Well, we'd love to, but you know ... some people frown at things like this in this part of the world."

Desmond nodded. "I know."

Ruth spoke again, "But we plan to do whatever will work for us and make us happy. Our happiness is what matters."

Desmond nodded again in agreement.

"We also plan to have a child or two with time."

"A child or two?" Desmond was clearly surprised.

Ruth laughed. "Yes."

"How? Through adoption?"

"That's an option."

"Wow! Is that kind of arrangement allowed by the government?"

Ruth shrugged nonchalantly. "Not really, but we know how to go about it or Linda could get pregnant somehow."

"Linda? Wow!" That was another confirmation to Desmond that Ruth was the male figure in the relationship.

Ruth chuckled again, feeling very much in control of her life.

"Linda also wants that?" Desmond couldn't help asking.

Ruth nodded, smiling. "Sure. We have talked about it."

They talked for about two minutes more and then Desmond left.

When Ruth returned to the living room, Linda called out to her from the kitchen.

"Are you ready to eat now?"

"Yes, please." Ruth answered.

Ruth joined Linda in the kitchen to assist her, and soon, they were seated at the dining table. As they ate dinner— rice and fish stew that was garnished with vegetables—they talked.

At about ten, Linda who had been watching TV while Ruth worked on her laptop, got up and announced that she was going to the bedroom to sleep.

"I'll join you soon." Ruth said.

Some minutes after, she stopped what she was doing and shut down the laptop. She checked the front door to ensure it was locked, switched off the light in the living room, and went inside the bedroom.

The medium size room with a built-in closet and white ceiling fan had photos of Ruth and Linda all over its cream-colored walls. The queen-size bed with three pillows was on a side of the room with some space between it and the wall. The room also had a dresser, a chair, a wall clock, two bedside tables, and a carpet that matched the wall color.

Ruth showered, wore her pyjamas, and then joined Linda in bed to cuddle up. They eventually slept around midnight.

She Who Has a Man | Taiwo Iredele Odubiyi

# CHAPTER 2

At about three in the morning, Ruth woke up to use the toilet, returned to bed, and went back to sleep.

Not too long after, she suddenly woke up troubled, with her heart racing. She'd had a dream. She reached out, took her phone from her bedside table, and checked the time. It was four-twenty.

She returned the phone and began to wonder about the dream.

The dream had started off ordinary—someone was chasing her and she was running away. While trying to escape, she saw her late paternal grandfather and happily ran in his direction. Then she suddenly remembered that he was dead and she turned away, in another direction.

Dreaming about dead people or being chased by someone or an animal was not strange to Ruth. If she was being chased, she always managed to escape or woke up from the dream at that point. Such dreams happened a lot, and no matter how bad the dream was, she was not bothered much and she soon forgot about it.

However, this seemingly ordinary dream suddenly took a dark turn. She saw herself and four friends, including Linda, walking in a direction and suddenly, an evil looking man appeared. He was holding a gun. Ruth and Linda ran in a direction while the other friends followed a different direction. Ruth and Linda heard footsteps behind them and when they looked back and saw the man, they stopped running. They held their hands up to show that they did not have weapons and would cooperate with him, but the man fired a shot. Linda fell and died.

Screaming, Ruth laid on the ground with her hands behind her, to show surrender. She expected the man to spare her life and take her away captive, but he shot at her too. For some seconds, she thought she was dead but when she realized that she was not, she chose to be quiet so the man would think she was dead and walk away. He did not walk away however and she began to wonder what he was doing. She didn't have to wonder for long. Suddenly she could feel the heat of fire and quickly raising her head, she looked, and saw that the man had started a fire. What was his plan?!

It soon became a large fire and the heat was unbearable. As she cried, begging the evil man for mercy, she doubted that he had any iota of mercy in him. When she saw the man approaching her, she screamed in terror for help.

Suddenly, a man dressed in white appeared and told her that she could be delivered from the evil man if she would do some things.

"It is not too late." The man in white added in a pleading way.

"What do I need to do? How can I be delivered from him?" Ruth found herself asking as she trembled all over.

"Believe in the Lord Jesus and you shall be saved." The man in white answered.

Ruth suddenly woke up at that point, terrified.

*What just happened?* She wondered in the darkness of the room as she recalled the dream. Somehow, this dream was different, and she hadn't been this terrified about a dream since she was a child.

*Believe in the Lord Jesus and you shall be saved?!*
*Jesus?!*

What was her business with Jesus? What did that statement mean? *And saved from what precisely?!* Frozen in terror, she tried to find answers to these questions.

Most of what she knew about Jesus was what she heard from people and saw on TV. As a young child, she'd followed her mother a few times to some churches for events, and she had sat beside her mother, playing, while service was going on. And as an adult, she'd attended church twice and then stayed away altogether.

What kind of dream was this? Why was the heat of the fire so unbearable? As she thought about the dream, she wondered who the evil man was. Was that the devil or a man in her life that she would need to stay away from?

And why had the dream seemed so real and terrifying? It was worse than anything she'd seen in a horror movie.

Taking a deep breath, she adjusted herself, moved closer to Linda, and prepared to sleep back.

Just then, Linda woke up. She got up, used the toilet, and returned to bed.

"Did I wake you up?" Linda asked when she saw that Ruth was awake.

"No, I was already awake. I had a bad dream." Ruth revealed.

"A bad dream?"

"Yes. I saw y-" Ruth stopped. She didn't think she should say that it was her she saw in the dream. She began again, "Someone was shot dead."

"Did you see the person's face?" Linda wanted to know.

"No." Ruth lied.

Linda pulled her close. "Pay no attention to it. We all have foolish dreams now and then. Dreams mean nothing."

"You're right."

"If every dream has meaning, I'd be in big trouble." Linda said and chuckled. "I've had all manners of dreams. Don't worry about it."

Ruth thanked Linda and closed her eyes. She was the strong one in the relationship and she must remain strong, she told herself. It was just a dream anyway, she reasoned.

For some time, she couldn't go back to sleep, but she eventually did, and woke up around seven-thirty in the morning, alone in the bed. Linda was not in sight. There was no movement in the apartment and that was when she remembered that Linda had a business appointment with someone.

Ruth would need to go out soon as well. She needed to buy some clothes and groceries, but she must be back at home by three in the afternoon so she could edit the pictures she snapped at a birthday ceremony on Sunday.

However, she remained in bed and tried to gather her thoughts together. The details and terror of the dream still filled her mind, and to her surprise, she still felt shaken.

She turned on the small flat-screen TV that hung on a wall of the room, and then took her phone to check if she had some messages she would need to respond to. There were indeed some chats and e-mails that needed her attention and she began to type her reply.

When she finished, she glanced at the time—it was now eight-thirty-five. She still had time to relax since she planned to get up at nine.

She looked at the TV—the channel was about news around the world—and the newscaster was talking about how a lady in America had been rescued from her abusive boyfriend. The lady had taken her dog to the vet office for a health check with the boyfriend. There, she managed to secretly slip a note to one of the workers. The worker read it and showed it to her colleague to read.

*Call the cops. My boyfriend is threatening me. He has a gun. Please don't let him know.*

Realizing the seriousness and danger of the situation, the workers acted immediately. They quietly alerted the cops, and then asked the couple to wait in a room, without making the man suspicious. About fifteen minutes after, some police officers arrived. They went to the room, arrested the man, and took his gun. As soon as some of the officers left the room with the boyfriend, the lady burst into tears and told the remaining officers how the boyfriend had held her captive in her home for two days. She also showed them the bruises on her body.

As Ruth watched, she couldn't help shaking her head at the wickedness of the man. She was happy for the lady. She admired the lady's fast thinking and courage to get help, and how the workers took action immediately without panicking. She wondered what she would have done if she were in the lady's shoes. Well, she might never know; that might never happen to her since she was the male figure in her relationship, she concluded.

The next news was about a family house that a man's ex set on fire in France because the man ended their relationship. Fortunately, the occupants were not hurt, but the house was fully engulfed in flames by the time the fire fighters and the police arrived.

The burning house was shown on TV and as Ruth watched it, she remembered the fire in her dream, and she could still see the face of the evil man in her mind. Troubled, she turned off the TV and got up. Within minutes, she'd had her bath and dressed in men's clothes and shoes. She usually wore men's clothes, but wore women's pant suit or blouse on jeans to places where she was expected to dress feminine.

At about ten-twenty, Ruth got into her car and pulled out of the compound. It had rained for the greater part of yesterday, but today was beautiful and sunny. As she sped toward the clothing store, with the windows up and the air conditioner on, she forgot all about the dream.

The traffic was light and she soon reached the store. Inside, she went to the men's section and picked a pair of jeans and two beautifully-made shirts.

She paid, left, and went to some other stores to buy groceries. Out of the corner of her eye, she saw two market women looking at her and talking. She could guess what they were talking about but she didn't care. How she lived was her business and she didn't have to answer to anyone.

She bought the groceries and put them on the back seat of her car. She was about to start the car when Linda called to know where she was and if she had bought groceries. Ruth informed her that she had, and was on her way back home.

She Who Has a Man | Taiwo Iredele Odubiyi

# CHAPTER 3

As Tokunbo Tomori walked briskly across the mirrored lobby of the second floor of *Divine Rest Guest House* toward his father's office that Tuesday afternoon, his shoes were soundless on the carpeted floor. The thirty-year-old man who wore glasses was dark in complexion and of an average height. He had short hair and short beard.

He and the manager of the Guest House were to have a meeting with his father, Seyi Tomori, the owner of the Guest House.

The Guest House, which was just off a big shopping mall, was established seven years ago and doing well. Seyi Tomori became a Christian about ten years ago and had decided to establish the Guest House to meet the needs of Christians. Tokunbo, an Economics University graduate, had resigned from where he was working last year to come on board as a director.

For about three years, his father had been inviting him to work for him and eventually take over the running of the business since Tokunbo was the man's only surviving son. His only daughter was a medical doctor.

He'd also promised to match the salary that Tokunbo was being paid where he worked. The proposal made sense and seemed like the right thing to do, but Tokunbo knew that God's leading was more important.

When he eventually felt convinced last year to do what his father wanted, his father's joy knew no bounds. God had answered another prayer—the beautiful Guest House would not end up being in the hands of a stranger. His own son would take over from him.

Tokunbo also had reasons to be grateful to God. He did not lack anything. He lived at home with his parents, had a good car, and had his own money. He was also certain that he was at the center of the will of God.

The Guest House had a modern design and security men at its two gates. It had eighteen rooms and suites, a large hall, and two small halls which were rented out to Christians for various events including church services. The church that Tokunbo and his family attended opened a new parish about eight months ago, using one of the two small halls for services.

There were two shops in the lobby on the ground floor: one sold jewelries, shoes and bags, while the other sold Christian books and Bibles.

Tokunbo reached his father's office, tapped briefly on the door, and turned the knob. His father and the manager, Alex, were there, and he greeted them. Alex, who had BA in Hotel Management, spoke fluent English, Yoruba,

Hausa, Igbo, and a little Spanish. This had impressed Tokunbo and made him to start learning French online.

Soon, the meeting started with a short prayer by Tokunbo's father, and then they began to discuss. The purpose of the monthly meeting was to review the business' performance, discuss policies, and talk about how to move the business forward.

When it was time for suggestions, Tokunbo said, "A couple will be arriving this weekend for their honeymoon."

"Their honeymoon? That should be my friend's daughter." Tokunbo's father said. "She's made reservations for a suite, right?"

"Yes, but I'm talking about another couple. I'd like to suggest that when we have couples on honeymoon, or a guest who is celebrating his or her birthday, we should give them a gift."

The manager nodded in agreement.

"I think it's okay. I have no objection." His father said. "I also think that whoever will deliver the gift should inform them that a church holds services in one of the halls, in case they'd like to attend while here."

"Okay, but they should not be forced to attend though." Tokunbo said.

"No, no. It's not by force." His father agreed.

When the meeting eventually ended an hour and a half after, Tokunbo and the manager left.

Back in his office, Tokunbo took his phone and found over one hundred messages waiting for him on WhatsApp. Most of the messages were in the group chat of his university classmates. The members of the group chatted a lot, and with a smile, he wondered what got them excited to chat so much today.

He called the kitchen and asked one of the male workers, who was also a member of his church, to bring his lunch.

While waiting for the food, he went on WhatsApp, and opened the group chat to see if there was something he would need to respond to. He did not chat much in the group but only responded to celebrations and important information, and he posted prayers on the first day of a new month.

Half of the members were not Christians, and so they posted all kinds of things. One of them, Ruth, was a lesbian, and flaunted it. Last week, she posted that a member shared the same birthday with her girlfriend, Linda, and when she posted a picture of the girlfriend, some of the members congratulated her. She often posted things to convince the members that her lifestyle was right. He did not respond to her posts but prayed for her and her lesbian partner that they would encounter God. When his church had an event last year, he had forwarded an invitation privately to all the members, including Ruth. She had replied that she was not interested and did not forget to tell him what he could do with his Jesus and church.

Tokunbo checked the chats and found that one of the male members who got married last year announced that his wife gave birth to a set of twins. Also, it was the birthday of three of the members.

Tokunbo began to type, congratulating and praying for these members. Afterward, he closed the group chat and began to check his other messages.

He would have loved to exit the WhatsApp group but somehow, he didn't think that he should. He couldn't condemn Ruth and the others in the group who were not Christians though. He used to be an alcoholic and lived a reckless life which resulted in two sons by two women. He had problems but didn't even know how to come out until he encountered God. What everyone needed was God.

Soon, his food was brought. He blessed it and as he ate, he continued using his phone. He created a group on WhatsApp for his church parish's welfare department since he was the head of the department. Adding the six members of the department to it, he welcomed them to the platform, and informed them that there was a need for them to have a brief meeting after the midweek service in the evening of that day.

*********

At home, while Linda prepared lunch, Ruth sat at her work table, doing some work on the images she'd captured at a birthday ceremony on Sunday on her laptop. As she looked at some couples in the pictures, she wondered if she and Linda could find a way to legalize their relationship. *We're okay the way we are though*, she thought. And then she frowned, *but why can't we do what heterosexual couples do?*

When food was ready, they ate and afterward, Ruth returned to her table.

About three hours after, Linda came to check on her progress. Then she went to the kitchen and came out with two glasses of drinks. Coming over, she put one down in front of Ruth.

"Ah, thank you." Ruth said and smiled at her. "Just what I needed."

Carrying the cup, she drank almost half of the drink before she stopped and put the cup down.

As she continued her work on the laptop, she did not remember the dream. However, much later in bed at night, it returned to her. The horror of the dream still overwhelmed her mind and she had the feeling that it was not an ordinary dream. If it was indeed a dream with meaning, how would she know it?

She decided that she would mention the dream to someone—someone she could confide in—with the hope that doing so would make her feel better.

Better still, she hoped the person would be able to interpret the dream for her. But where could she find such a person? She thought about the people she was close to—

that she considered to be her friends—but she didn't think any of them would be able to help her.

It occurred to her to talk to someone who was a Christian. *Those Christians talk as if they have some form of supernatural power and a God Who answers prayers*, she thought. If they did, she'd like to talk to one of them, as she had questions begging for answers.

Her mind went to a professional colleague who was a Christian, but she was not really close to the person.

A Christian? Some members of her University WhatsApp group were Christians, and she wondered if she should talk to one of them.

If she would, who among them? She began to consider the members who were Christians, but she dismissed them one after the other. Her mind went to Tokunbo, but she dismissed him too. They might see it as an opportunity to preach to her, and she didn't want that. Besides, she wasn't sure that she'd want to expose her personal life to any of them.

Who else did she know to be a Christian? Any family member?

Ah, Rachel, her younger sister. She was a Christian. Good.

She settled for Rachel. She'd talk to Rachel. She'd like to know what Rachel thought about the dream, and if Rachel said something she didn't like, she could ask her to shut up. She could handle Rachel.

Since she would be going to deliver a photo book to someone tomorrow, Ruth decided that she would stop at Rachel's store which was not far from her parents' house. The right thing would be for her to send a message to Rachel now, so she could expect her tomorrow. However, knowing that Rachel might tell their mother, and their mother might ask her to stop at the family house, which she wouldn't want to do, Ruth decided to spring a surprise on Rachel.

The next day, Wednesday, after delivering the photo book around eleven in the morning, she called Rachel to know where she was at the moment.

Rachel said she was in her store.

"Okay. Send your address to me. I'm coming over now." Ruth told her.

"Coming over?" Rachel was surprised.

Ruth had not been to the store since Rachel got it. She had stayed away when Rachel told her that it was given to her by her church.

Rachel spoke again, "Is everything okay?"

"Yes, unless you consider it a sin or crime for me to visit my sister," Ruth said with a smile evident in her voice.

Rachel chuckled. "No, I'm just surprised. I'm in the store. I'll send the address to you right away."

Twenty-seven-year-old Rachel had picked up interest in and started making beaded jewelry on the side while studying Journalism in university. The business idea started when she saw Ruth go into photography, and like Ruth, the interest quickly became a passion that created a new path in life for her as orders were coming in.

She had given her life to Jesus in her final year of university at a campus crusade that was organized by one of the campus fellowships. After her graduation and NYSC, she returned to her parents' house and joined *The Believers Church,* which was just about a twenty-minute drive from the house.

She did not bother to look for a job but went into her business full-time, and began to work from home. Fortunately for her, the church built six stores on a side of the compound last year, with entrance doors that opened to the street. One of the stores was used as the church's bookstore while the other five were given to church members with growing businesses. They were to use the space for three years after which they would vacate, to allow some other church members to have the same opportunity. Rachel was one of the fortunate five people. Her business was growing, and she now had a lady who assisted her.

Ruth got the address within a minute and headed to the place. When she reached the street named *Church Street,* she continued driving until she got to *The Believers Church,* popularly called *TBC*, which was at the end of the long street. She looked at the stores and drove on slowly until she saw the signboard, *Rachel's Place.* She parked right in front of it and got down, with her camera hanging around her neck.

Opening the glass door of the store, she stepped inside the air-conditioned room.

Rachel stopped what she was doing, got up, and greeted Ruth warmly. Her staff member also greeted Ruth, even though she didn't know who Ruth was to Rachel.

Ruth sat down on a chair, and Rachel offered her a bottle of cold water which she accepted.

After some small talk, Ruth told her sister that she'd like to discuss a matter with her.

"Okay. Er," Rachel looked at her staff member. The lady was working on an order. Rachel didn't think she should stop the lady by asking her to excuse them.

"Okay, let's go outside to talk." She decided.

Outside, Ruth suggested that they sit inside her car, and they did.

"Is everything okay?" Rachel wanted to know.

"Yes, I just want to know your opinion about something." Ruth answered, and then carefully, she began, "Do you think that some dreams have meaning?"

Rachel nodded. "Yes, some dreams—not all dreams."

*Not all dreams. Hmm.*

"What happened? Did you have a dream?" Rachel probed.

Slowly, Ruth nodded.

"Tell me about it."

"It was a foolish dream, really, but ..." Ruth hesitated.

"Tell me about it." Rachel said again in an encouraging way.

"Okay. I had the dream in the early hours of Tuesday." Ruth began, and then she told her sister all about it, with all the details still clear in her mind.

"Hmm, that was not an ordinary dream." Rachel said when Ruth stopped.

"You think so?"

Rachel nodded. "I know so."

"Okay. So?"

Rachel opened her mouth to talk, and then stopped. What would God want her to do? She quickly considered it, and changed her mind—she didn't think she should be the one to talk to Ruth. Ruth could be very difficult, and might not even allow her to say much to properly counsel her. Besides, this dream was not an ordinary one. It was a message to Ruth, and as such, this must be handled carefully. It would be better that she took Ruth to her pastor.

"I'd like to take you to my pastor." Rachel said and pointed to the church compound.

"Huh?" Ruth frowned. "Your pastor?! For what?!"

"I think he'd be able to explain things better."

Ruth shook her head adamantly and said firmly, "No, I'm not seeing your pastor or any pastor!"

"You need to see my pastor, he's around. He's in his office and he will attend to you. It's important." Rachel told her.

"No. I'm not seeing any pastor." Ruth insisted. "Tell me your opinion about the dream, that's all."

"No, you need to see my pastor. He will be able to interpret the dream correctly and answer whatever questions you may have about it." Rachel equally insisted.

Ruth stared at her for some seconds, trying to gauge her sincerity. *Was this indeed necessary?*

She sighed and thought about it—had she not come to know the meaning of the dream? If the pastor was in his office and could help, then she might have to see him. What could it hurt?

She reluctantly agreed. "I hope this won't take long."

"It shouldn't." Rachel said.

"Meaning?"

Rachel smiled. "It shouldn't take long."

"Don't let it take long. I have things to do." Ruth said rudely.

Rachel took her phone, and as she called the pastor, Ruth looked on.

"Good morning, Daddy."

Ruth frowned. *Daddy?! Why would Rachel call him that?* She didn't hear the pastor's response, but Rachel said - thank you, sir.

Rachel went on. "My sister is here with me. She had a dream and I think she needs to see you for proper counseling, sir. I don't know if I can bring her now ... okay Daddy ... yes sir ... thank you sir."

Rachel ended the call and looked at Ruth, "Okay, let's go."

With a scowl on her face, Ruth alighted from the car, locked the doors and followed her sister.

When they entered the church compound through the pedestrian gate, Ruth saw two buildings painted white, one was small and the other was big and rectangular in shape. They walked toward the small building which had some doors and she guessed that it was the administrative building. The bigger building was obviously the church auditorium.

Rachel led her to a door, pushed it open, and held it for her.

As Ruth followed Rachel inside the office, she told herself that she would have a good laugh with Linda when she returned home and told her about this.

There, they saw a young man seated behind a desk, reading a book. Rachel greeted him familiarly and said that the pastor was expecting them.

The man whom Ruth guessed was the pastor's personal assistant, asked Rachel to give him a minute. Getting up, he walked to an adjoining door, opened it, and entered.

He returned almost immediately and asked them to go in. He held the pastor's office door open for them.

"Thank you." Rachel said.

Ruth did not talk as she followed her sister inside the pastor's office. *Why should I thank him? I didn't ask to be brought here.*

The pastor, who was dark in complexion, was of an average height, and Ruth guessed that he must be in his late forties. Why would Rachel call him Daddy when their father was much older than him? Ruth hoped she would not be expected to call him Daddy because she would not.

Rachel greeted the pastor while Ruth looked at him with suspicion. She knew she was supposed to greet him, but she didn't want to, and she liked to please herself as much as possible.

But the pastor looked at her and greeted her.

Suddenly, Ruth began to feel uneasy and nervous, which she could not explain. She had to force herself to calm down by glancing around the air-conditioned, cream-colored room, taking in her surroundings. Three padded armed guest chairs faced the pastor's black executive table and on the large table were a big Bible, a laptop, an iPad, two cell phones, a framed photo of his family, a box of tissue, a book, and a name plate that read – Pastor Joel Dominic. A bookshelf was in a corner by the pastor's black leather armed-chair while two comfortable couches and a small glass table were on a side of the room. The room also had a TV and a painting that matched the gray rug on the floor and the window curtains.

"Daddy, this is my sister, Ruth." Rachel told the pastor.

"Your sister?"

"Yes, Daddy." Rachel confirmed.

Pastor Joel looked from Rachel to Ruth. Rachel had told him some time last year that she had an older sister—a photographer—who was a lesbian. And as he looked at Ruth now, with the camera hanging on her neck, the way she dressed, and her cocky attitude, he knew that this was the sister.

"How are you?" He asked warmly, not at all upset that Ruth did not greet him.

"I'm fine." Ruth forced herself to say. *A pastor? What have I gotten myself into?*

"Praise God!" The pastor said. "Please sit down."

"Thank you, sir." Rachel said.

They sat on two of the chairs that faced the pastor's table.

Pastor Joel leaned forward and looked at Rachel, "So, you said that your sister would like to discuss with me."

"Yes." Rachel said.

Leaning forward a little, she told him that Ruth had had a dream, and that she'd told Ruth that the pastor would be able to explain things better to her.

"Alright. What was the dream about?" Pastor Joel looked from Rachel to Ruth.

"Go ahead." Rachel encouraged Ruth to talk.

Ruth did and when she stopped, the pastor confirmed what Rachel had earlier told her—it was not an ordinary dream.

"What the man in white told you is straight from the Bible, in the book of the Acts of the Apostles."

Taking his Bible, he opened it to chapter sixteen of the Acts of the apostles, and then pushed the Bible toward Ruth. "Please read from verse twenty nine to thirty one." He told her.

Reluctantly, Ruth brought the Bible closer and looked at it. "Where are the verses? I can't find-"

Rachel moved close, showed her the verses, and moved back.

Ruth began to read. "Then he called for a light, ran in, and fell down trembling before Paul and Silas. And he brought them out and said, 'Sirs, what must I do to be saved?' So they said, 'Believe on the Lord Jesus Christ, and you will be saved, you and your household.'"

*Wow! So, it's in the Bible!*

"Does that seem like your conversation with the man in your dream?" Pastor Joel asked Ruth.

Ruth slowly nodded as she pushed the Bible back to the pastor. Okay, so it was in the Bible, but what she'd like to know was the relevance of the dream to her.

The pastor began by explaining the event in the scripture, and then he went on to interpret Ruth's dream, what the words of the man in Ruth's dream meant, and how Ruth could be saved. He explained that everyone was born a sinner and needed the Savior—Jesus Christ—to be saved, so they would not end up in hell.

He also told her about Jesus, how much He loved her, and that He was trying to get her attention. "He died on the cross for you."

He showed her more scriptures and then asked if she would want to become saved by praying and accepting Jesus as her personal Lord and Savior.

*Why would I want to do that?!* Ruth thought. If she was chatting with him on WhatsApp, she would have used the 'eye roll' emoji "🙄" to express her disdain, annoyance, and disbelief at the suggestion. *Accept Jesus?!*

She shook her head and said no.

Surprised and disappointed, Rachel's mouth dropped open which Ruth ignored.

Pastor Joel tried to persuade Ruth to accept Jesus as Lord by briefly sharing his salvation experience, but when it was obvious that she was not interested in doing so, he decided to pray for her and commit her into God's hands.

As he began to pray, he did not hear any sound from Ruth, only Rachel said Amen. He opened his eyes and when he saw Ruth glancing around his office with a frown on her face, he asked her to close her eyes and say Amen.

She closed her eyes.

The pastor closed his eyes and continued praying for Ruth while both Ruth and Rachel said Amen.

He asked God to reveal Himself to Ruth, and make His will come to pass in her life.

"In Jesus' name I pray."

"Amen." Ruth and Rachel said in unison.

# CHAPTER 4

Ruth and Rachel eventually left, and as they walked toward the gate, Ruth told Rachel not to say anything to their parents about her visit.

"Well, let's hope they don't ask me anything, because if they do, I'll have to tell them the truth. I'm not going to lie." Rachel said.

Ruth looked at her with a scowl. "Why would they ask you about my visit? How will they know that I visited you if you don't tell them? I'm simply telling you to mind your business!" She hissed.

Rachel was tempted to insult Ruth, but she took a deep breath to control herself instead. Ruth was supposed to appreciate what she did, but apparently, she did not. She did not even say thank you to Pastor Joel when they were leaving his office. Why did Ruth have such a bad attitude?

Rachel changed the subject by encouraging Ruth to give all that the pastor told her a thought, and to contact her if necessary.

But Ruth did not respond, and when they reached her car, she simply said goodbye, opened the car and got in.

On the way home, Ruth was thinking about all that happened. If someone had told her that she would sit to listen to the words of a pastor, read the Bible, and say Amen to a pastor's prayers, she would have asked the person – *What have you been drinking? That can never happen!*

But it had happened. And worse—she'd like to brush off his words but some of them had penetrated her heart and lodged themselves in it.

She smiled as she remembered the moment that the pastor asked if she'd like to become a Christian. If it had not been pathetic, she would have said it was funny. How could she become a Christian? That was the last thing she would do! That would never happen.

*Me?! Become a Christian?! No way*! As a Christian, she would have to read the Bible, go to church, pray, and follow a set of rules. No, she couldn't do that. She wasn't cut out for such a life.

Besides, she did not like to follow rules. She always had problems with her mother while at home. She was a rebel at heart and she liked it that way. It was one of the reasons she liked and chose photography. With photography, she could express her opinion and do her thing her way while making money. She hated control. It was also the reason she had also dabbled in smoking and drinking, although occasionally. The only thing she did not do was drugs. One of her previous partners had tried to introduce her to it, but she had refused.

She remembered the pastor's prayer and wondered if Jesus was really real—the pastor had prayed as if Jesus was real and present with them in the office.

She didn't think Jesus was real though. Deciding to test Jesus, she said, "Jesus, I don't know, but if You are real, show Yourself to me ... talk to me."

Nothing happened. Thunder did not strike her dead and there was no voice. Nothing. That confirmed her thought—Jesus was not real, she concluded.

Linda came to her mind. She would have loved to discuss the meeting with the pastor with Linda so they could have a good laugh about it as they usually did, but somehow, she wasn't sure she should tell her. Discussing with Linda would mean revealing that Linda was the one who was shot dead in the dream, but she did not want that.

Besides, Linda might blame her for agreeing to see the pastor, but she had done it because the scary dream was about them both.

What would telling Linda achieve anyway? It wasn't as if she would be able to do anything about the bad dream. Aside that, Linda was emotionally fragile and easily upset. She wouldn't like to bother her.

With that settled, Ruth slotted a CD into the CD player and began to hum to the music that filled the inside of the car, so that she could forget the words of the pastor.

Her phone began to ring, and when she saw that it was Rachel calling, she hissed and ignored the shrill ringing. Why was Rachel calling her? To preach to her or what? Had she not done enough damage to her emotions? A couple would be coming to her house at six in the evening for a photoshoot, and she needed a clear mind to do a good job. However, her mind had been thrown into a turmoil—courtesy of Rachel, she thought and hissed.

Linda was at home and after lunch, Ruth went to the bedroom to rest not only her body but also her mind. The alarm woke her up at four and she came to the living room. With the help of Linda, she arranged the living room, and set up her camera, lighting, and other necessary things.

The couple arrived on time. Ruth had asked them to bring necessities and without delay, she set to work, with music playing softly in the background. They eventually finished around nine-forty-five and the couple left.

Later in bed, fresh thoughts about the day began to seep into her mind and she began to play back in her mind some of the things that the pastor said about Jesus. Taking her phone, she went on YouTube and typed Jesus. She wanted to see what would come up. Several videos did. *Really?! Why? What is special about Jesus?!* She wondered as she closed YouTube and put her phone down. She took a book and began to read until she fell asleep.

**********

Tokunbo got to the office early on Monday morning, April 27. He responded to some e-mails and chats, made some calls, and afterward, had a meeting with a pastor who wanted to hold a retreat for his ministers in the Guest House.

At about one-thirty in the afternoon, he left his office and went to the restaurant which was on the ground floor of the Guest House. He wanted to meet the guests that might be there as he usually did, to know how they were enjoying their stay and to resolve any problem they might have. Eight of the tables were occupied. He was about to go to one of them when loud laughter from a table caught his attention. He looked in the direction and saw a man and a lady at the table, talking and laughing as they ate. He had a feeling that they were the couple on honeymoon and he went over.

With a big smile, he introduced himself.

"We're pleased to meet you." The man told him. "My name is Chris, and this is my wife, Stella. We're on our honeymoon."

Tokunbo congratulated the couple, and thanked them for choosing the Guest House for their honeymoon. When he asked if they were having a nice experience in the Guest House, they answered in the affirmative.

"Great!" He responded. "I have a small gift for you, courtesy of the Guest House."

"Really? Oh, wow!"

"A member of the staff will bring it to your room when you return there."

Stella and Chris thanked him.

He asked if this was their first time at the Guest House and when they said yes, he wanted to know how they got to know about the place.

"A friend told me that a couple was here on their honeymoon in December, and they said that they had a great time." Stella said.

Tokunbo chuckled. "In December?"

"Yes." She mentioned their names.

"Oh, I remember them—Sarah and Francis." Tokunbo responded.

"This is a nice place."

"Thank you. A Pentecostal church holds services in one of the halls, in case you'd like to physically attend church while you're here."

Stella said that her friend mentioned it to her, and they intended to join the church to worship God.

Back in his office about an hour and a half later, Tokunbo asked a staff member to take the gift to them.

**********

About two weeks after, on Sunday morning, May 10, Ruth had another dream. This time, she saw a Man who told her, "I am the Way, the Truth, and the Life. I am

Jesus." Suddenly, glorious light surrounded Him and some people bowed to worship Him.

Ruth woke up, and as she remembered the dream, she frowned. *Jesus again?! What was going on?* Was there something she was doing that was bringing these dreams?

Afraid of having another dream that would bother her, she refused to sleep back. She took her phone to watch a movie but eventually slept off.

She woke up much later and, while having breakfast of sliced bread and fried egg with Linda, she used her phone. As she was searching for a movie to watch on YouTube, one of the videos suggested by YouTube was about Jesus.

Realising that the suggestion was because she searched for Jesus recently on YouTube, she went to her watch history on YouTube and removed the videos about Jesus that she had clicked on.

*Jesus!* Her mind went to her dream and as she thought about it, she wondered if this second dream was related to the first one. And what did *the way, the truth, and the life* mean?

When Linda went to the bathroom, Ruth quickly called Rachel. When she said that she had another dream, Rachel encouraged her to come over.

"I'll come tomorrow." Ruth told her. *Let's hear what that pastor has to say this time.*

At night, she was almost afraid to fall asleep, but she eventually did, and dreamed about fighting with someone.

When she woke up in the morning and remembered the dream, she took a deep breath. She knew that it wasn't a good dream, more so as she did not have victory in the dream. However, it did not bother her as much as the dream about the evil man and the one about Jesus.

At about ten, she left the house, got to Rachel's store, and together they went to Pastor Joel's office.

"That's right out of the Bible." The pastor told Ruth after hearing the details of the dream.

*From the Bible again*?! Was Jesus indeed trying to talk to her? Ruth wondered with a frown, feeling perplexed.

Opening his Bible to John chapter fourteen verse six, the pastor showed the verse to Ruth, and asked her to read it.

She did. "*Jesus said to him, "I am the way, the truth, and the life. No one comes to the Father except through Me."*

As she returned the Bible to him, she said, "I'd like to know if there's something I'm doing that's making me have these dreams."

"Well, it's not so much about what you're doing but about what God is doing. He is trying to reveal Himself to you ... the two dreams are very direct and scriptural."

Ruth's frown deepened. Could that be true? Why would God be doing that?

The pastor went on. "However, I need to warn you ... not all dreams are from God and as such, everyone needs to be careful. Some dreams are demonic. This means that satan can give dreams which is why the Bible warns us in First

John chapter four verse one to test the spirits to see if they are from God, and to be on guard against spirits that deceive, distort, and distract. Dreams can also come through much activity, according to Ecclesiastes chapter five verse three. This means that dreams could come as a result of your activities, and what you watch or read."

*I haven't been watching or reading anything religious,* Ruth thought.

The pastor continued, "God speaks to us today through His word which is the Bible, and His Spirit. However, He can give a dream or vision to say something to someone, probably to reveal His will or to warn the person of impending danger."

"So, my two dreams are from God?"

"Yes, I believe so, and I will explain. A dream from God will completely agree with what is written in the Bible. God will never contradict Himself for He is not the Author of confusion. He will never send a dream that contradicts what is recorded in the Bible. No dream or vision that goes directly against what is written in the Bible is from God."

Ruth took a deep breath.

"Also, if a dream is from God, He will make the meaning clear somehow. He will make sure that the message is clearly understood. If it's not very clear, the person should pray about it and move on."

As Ruth listened to him, she tried to make sense of what God seemed to be doing in her life.

"About your dreams, I don't know why God has decided to use dreams to get your attention. However, that is what He has done. He is definitely revealing His will to you, to rescue you … to help you."

"But why?"

The pastor smiled. "Because He loves you. The Bible says *For God so loved the world that He gave His only begotten Son that whosoever believes in Him should not perish but have eternal life*. There's nothing God cannot do to get a particular person's attention."

He went on to tell her of how God used the burning bush to get Moses' attention.

He continued counseling Ruth, and afterward, asked if she'd want to become a Christian. Again, she said no.

Shortly after, she and Rachel left.

"Why have you refused to accept Jesus as your Lord and Savior?" Rachel asked her, sounding perplexed.

"Please stop!" Ruth snapped. "Is it by force?"

"No, it's not, but tomorrow may be too late."

"Too late? … As in - I might die soon?" Ruth asked, and then relaxed her face and grinned. "No, no, that's not about to happen. I'm not dying anytime soon."

"Who told you that? What gives you that assurance?" Rachel glanced sideways at her.

"Do you wish for me to die soon?" Ruth shot back.

"No, God forbid! You will not die young in Jesus' name." Rachel prayed. "But only God knows when we will die. The point is that you need to give your life to Jesus, now."

Ruth cut her off. "Look, leave me alone! I'm fine. I don't need to be rescued. I don't even know what your pastor is talking about."

The next morning, Ruth was surprised when Rachel called and said she'd want to come to her house that day.

"To my house? Why?"

"It's just to see you." Rachel answered and hoped that Ruth's partner would not be at home. But even if she was, Rachel planned to be nice to her, discuss with Ruth, and leave. She might even share the word of God with the partner.

"Okay, come around three in the afternoon." Ruth said. Linda would have gone out by then as she wouldn't want Linda to hear whatever Rachel was coming to discuss.

When Rachel arrived at three-twenty, she did not see Linda. "Where's she?"

"She had to go out to run some errands."

*Good*, Rachel thought.

"Would you like something to drink?" Ruth asked.

"No. I won't stay long." Rachel answered and opening her handbag, she brought out a black book.

Ruth frowned. "What's that? A Bible?"

Rachel nodded. "Yes, I bought it for you." She put it on the side table in front of Ruth.

Ruth shook her head immediately. "No." *What made her think I'd need or read that thing?*

"Why not?"

"Are you kidding me?! One, it's too big. Two, I don't think that I need it."

"Okay, I'll take it back and get a small one for you. You need it." Rachel said.

Ruth rolled her eyes.

Rachel encouraged her briefly and prayed for her.

After she left, Ruth began to think. In the first dream, she had been told to change. What exactly did she need to change?! The photography job? She didn't think that God was against photography. She knew a professional photographer who was a Christian.

Then her mind went to her lifestyle and she wondered if that was the problem. Was being a lesbian okay with God? As she thought about it, she remembered all the people—Christians and non-Christians—who had condemned the practice and told her that she was wrong. She didn't think that God was okay with it, but how could it be wrong? She wondered.

Another thought occurred to her ... how could God be against the practice when He created her that way? She also remembered that at the age of about seven, a woman had made her watch a lesbian porn after which she molested her. She had told Ruth afterward that God made both of them that way and they did not have a choice. If indeed she did not have a choice, why would God or anyone condemn her?

Feeling both bothered and confused, she decided to ask the pastor for his opinion about lesbianism.

His opinion? No, she didn't want his opinion. She had an idea of what it would be. What she needed to know was God's opinion about it or if there was anything about it in the Bible. And if God was against it, why did He create her that way, and what did He expect her to do?

The next day, after her meeting with a client and visit to her barber's shop to cut her hair, she drove to Rachel's store.

Rachel was busy working on an urgent jewelry order and she asked Ruth to go and see the pastor alone.

"You think he'd attend to me without you being there?"

"Sure." Rachel assured her. "Better still, let me inform him that you're here to see him."

Rachel called the pastor on the phone and told him that Ruth would like to see him. When the call ended, she told Ruth, "You can go."

"Okay. Er ... what am I expected to call him ... Daddy or Pastor Joel?" Ruth asked. And then dismissed it. "Never mind." There was no way she would call him Daddy. He might be Rachel's Daddy, but he was not hers. She'd call him Pastor Joel or better still, she'd try not to call him anything. She'd do what she needed to do, and leave.

Deciding to answer Ruth's question anyway, Rachel shrugged and said, "Well, Daddy or ... Pastor, whichever one you're comfortable with." Ruth was not a member of the church, and definitely not a Christian. She didn't think that what Ruth called the pastor would matter much.

Ruth ignored what Rachel said and left to go inside the church compound. She saw the pastor's PA, told him that she was Rachel's sister, and that she would like to see 'Pastor'.

The PA went into the pastor's office to inform him and soon returned. Holding the pastor's door open, he told Ruth, "You can come in."

"Thank you." Ruth said to the PA as she passed him.

In the office, she greeted the pastor.

"Your sister said you'd like to discuss with me." Pastor Joel said.

Ruth nodded and then glanced back to be sure that the PA had gone and the door was closed.

The PA had returned to his office, but left the pastor's door wide open, to Ruth's surprise. Was it intentional? She wondered.

She returned her gaze to the pastor, and lowering her voice, she said, "Yes. Er ... I have a friend who is a lesbian, and we are wondering what God's opinion is about it."

"Okay." The pastor smiled. "God's opinion is that it is wrong, and your friend who is in a same-sex relationship— whether a male or female—should come out of it."

She Who Has a Man | Taiwo Iredele Odubiyi

Opening his Bible to Genesis chapter two, he read it from verse twenty one to twenty three.

Then he explained, "When God made a woman for the man, He knew what He was doing. He doesn't make a mistake. If God didn't mind same-sex relationship, He could have made a man for the man, Adam, to show His approval, and Adam could have called him Steve, not Eve. Or after making a woman for the man, God could have made another couple of the same sex, but no, God did neither because same-sex relationship was not what He wanted. As a matter of fact, in the Bible—Jeremiah chapter nineteen verse five—God said that some human beings do some things that He did not command or speak about. Those things never even came into His mind. It may seem natural, but it's not natural."

He read and explained some other scriptures that confirmed God's opinion.

Then he said, "I know that you said your friend is the lesbian ... but are you one too?"

Ruth wanted to lie, but the way he asked the question and the way he looked at her—as if he could see into her soul—made it difficult for her to lie.

Slowly, she nodded. And for the first time in a long time, she felt some embarrassment to admit it.

She expected to see condemnation in his eyes, but didn't.

The pastor simply smiled and nodded in understanding as he gazed steadily back at her. Then he said, "I was a drug addict but God saved me and transformed my life. He wants to do the same in your life, but the first step is to become a Christian by giving your life to Jesus. Doing so gives you a new heart which leads to a new nature, and subsequently gives you a new attitude to sin and a new behaviour."

"So, God wants me to be straight?"

"Yes, but He wants more than that. He wants your heart. He wants to save you, help you, bless you, and it's all because He loves you."

He paused to allow his words sink in. Then he added, "The problem is not just about lesbianism, it's about being a sinner. We were all born into sin, and every lie, rebellion, and sin deserves God's punishment. When we become a Christian, our lives change."

Ruth shifted uncomfortably in her seat. Then she asked, "How do I give my life to Jesus?"

"It's very simple ... you will need to pray and accept Jesus as your personal Lord and Savior, and then, begin to follow Him."

As Pastor Joel explained further, Ruth told herself that she wasn't ready for such life. What would she tell Linda? Her friends?

She eventually left the office without committing herself to God. It was just too hard to take that step.

Rachel was still busy. Ruth said goodbye and on the way home, she was thinking about all that the pastor said. *Maybe I have been wrong.*

Everything she knew and believed had been turned upside down. If it was true that God did not approve same-sex relationship, then it meant that she and Linda were wrong and in trouble. She had always been with a woman. What would having a man be like? She considered it and shook her head. She didn't want it! There would be many things to adjust in her life, and she didn't think she was ready for that. She couldn't.

Much later at night, as she got in bed with Linda, she felt confused. And for the first time, she felt that being in bed with her was not right.

Linda wanted intimacy, but Ruth shook her head. "Not tonight."

"Tired?"

"Yes." Ruth answered, although it was more in her emotions than her body.

And for some time, she couldn't sleep as her heart was heavy, thinking about different things.

## CHAPTER 5

Two days after, as Ruth prepared to go out, she felt lost. Even Linda had asked her twice if everything was okay, and she'd had to assure Linda that she was fine. But she was not fine—she didn't know who she was anymore.

Soon, she left the house in her car and entered the flow of traffic. The sun was shining brightly and the weather was hot. She wound up the windows and turned on the air-conditioner.

Still feeling confused and troubled, she decided to talk to Jesus and she said, "Jesus, if You can hear me, are You the One talking to me? Are you indeed trying to get my attention?"

She brought her car to a stop behind a car at a red light. Absentmindedly, she looked at the car, and noticed a sticker at its rear windshield. The sticker contained only a word—*Yes*.

Yes what?! Ruth wondered. Why would someone put such a sticker on a car? It didn't even make sense.

Suddenly the word struck her. *What*?! Could this be an answer to her questions? *Yes, I am the One talking to you.*

*Yes, I am indeed trying to get your attention.* Hmm. Somehow, she felt that it was the answer.

*Or am I losing my mind?! What's going on?!*

Her phone rang, cutting into her thoughts. It was one of her clients, and she pushed her concerns aside to focus on the business at hand.

\*\*\*\*\*\*\*\*\*\*

On the second day of June, Ruth woke up in the middle of the night with a start. She'd heard a voice in her dream that said *read the book of John and it will tell you about Me.*

*Book of John?* What was that? And more importantly, who was the 'Me'? Was there such a book, and if yes, where would she find it? Was this dream also about Jesus?!

She took her phone and sent a chat to Rachel.

*I had another dream.*

Almost immediately, there was a reply.

*I'll be in my store. Let's talk.*

Ruth typed.

*Ok. You haven't slept or what?*

*I woke up to pray for some minutes.*

Ruth typed.

*Ok. I'll see you later in the day.*

She slept back and woke up around seven. While Ruth did their laundry, Linda prepared breakfast. Ruth planned to leave the house at about ten to see a client. Linda would also be going out around in the afternoon to see a movie producer who had called and asked her to see him unfailingly that day.

Ruth's meeting with the client, a musician, went well. When she left, she drove to the church and got there around two in the afternoon. Only Rachel was in her store, as her assistant had gone out to make a supply.

Ruth told her sister, "I had another dream."

Rachel laughed and said, "Maybe you should change your name to Josephine."

Ruth smiled. "Why? Who is Josephine?"

"A man called Joseph in the Bible also had dreams. Josephine is the female name." Rachel explained.

"Well, I don't even know if it was actually a dream because I didn't see anything, no face - only a voice that said *read the book of John and it will tell you about Me.*

"Wow!" Rachel exclaimed. "Oh my God! You heard that?!"

Ruth frowned. "Yes. What's wrong?"

"You really did?"

"Yes,"

"Oh my God!" Rachel exclaimed again. "I'm having goose bumps right now."

Ruth frowned. "Why?"

"Because God loves you so much and is doing these things for you." Rachel answered.

Suddenly, she burst into tears.

Ruth was both surprised and scared. *What's going on?* "Why are you crying? Are you okay, Rachel?"

"Don't let God's grace be in vain in your life. God loves you." Rachel pleaded with Ruth.

In a sober voice, Ruth asked, "So, the voice was from God?"

"Yes, that was Jesus." Rachel confirmed and used the back of her hand to wipe her face.

"Jesus or God?"

"That was Jesus. However, Jesus is the Son of God, the second Person in Trinity, so He is also God."

Ruth did not understand the explanation, but went ahead to ask another question. "Which book is the book of John?"

Rachel explained that it was one of the books in the Bible that spoke about Jesus.

"Please go and see my pastor." Rachel encouraged her. "I'll join you if my assistant returns on time."

Ruth did, and Pastor Joel's PA promptly ushered her into his office, leaving the door open which Ruth noticed as she sat down on one of the visitors' chairs.

She told the pastor about the dream, and he said that the book of John gave an account of the ministry of Jesus.

While he was still explaining the dream to Ruth, Rachel came in, closed the door, and sat on a chair.

When the pastor finished talking, he asked Ruth if she'd like to give her life to Jesus.

When she took a deep breath and hesitated again, he asked her, "What's your concern?"

She took another deep breath before she asked, "What will I need to do to be a Christian? How am I expected to live?"

He answered her questions in detail, and then he asked again, "Will you give your life to Jesus now?"

She didn't think that she had a choice, and she nodded slowly.

"Thank You, Jesus!" The pastor exclaimed. "Say after me – Lord Jesus..."

"Lord Jesus..."

As the pastor led Ruth in prayer, tears of joy ran down Rachel's face.

And as Ruth gave her life to Jesus, peace came over her. She had several questions and concerns on her mind, but she felt that she had done the right thing.

Afterward, the pastor told her, "As I've been telling you, a person, especially a child of God should be careful about dreams. God simply chose to give you these dreams, but don't expect to keep having dreams. Don't believe all dreams and don't expect to be led by dreams. God leads His children by His word and His Spirit. Also, you will need to begin to read the Bible. It will make you know the will of God and how to live."

When he asked if she had a Bible that she could use, Rachel said she had bought one for her.

"Oh, splendid." The pastor responded, and then advised Ruth to start reading it from the book of John.

They were still talking when the door opened and a woman came in, holding a phone in her hand.

"Mummy," Rachel stood immediately to greet her.

"Rachel dear, God bless you." She responded.

Pastor Joel sat back, and smiling, he told the woman, "Darling, meet Rachel's sister, Ruth." And to Ruth, he said, "This is my wife, Pastor Ida."

Ruth stood and greeted her.

"I'm pleased to meet you." Pastor Ida told Ruth with a broad smile.

"She has just given her life to Jesus."

"Oh, praise God!" She exclaimed. "That's the best decision anyone could make."

Then she went to her husband. "The manager is on the phone. He'd like to say hello."

She gave the phone to the pastor. He talked on the phone for about a minute, returned the phone, and she left for her office.

Pastor Joel asked Ruth if she could wait to join the church's Bible study which would start in about two hours' time, at six.

"Bible study?" She asked and looked from the pastor to her sister.

"Yes, it's a collective study of the Bible," the pastor explained.

"I'll be there. It won't take long." Rachel assured her.

Ruth hesitated. Well, she could, but what would she tell Linda? She thought and then decided she would lie to Linda—tell her that she had to see some people for business or that there was heavy traffic.

"Okay." She agreed to attend the church service. *Me, Church? What have I done to myself?!*

Pastor Joel gave her his call card and his wife's, and said that she should not hesitate to call them if necessary.

When Ruth and Rachel left the pastor's office, Rachel made Ruth know that she had changed the Bible to a smaller one. "It's in my store. You need it so you can read the book of John."

They went to an eatery across the road and as they ate, they talked.

Back in Rachel's store, Ruth frowned when she saw the Bible. "I want something very small. Is there no smaller one? This is still big."

"There are smaller ones, but I'm not sure you will be able to read the words." Rachel pointed out.

When Ruth didn't take the Bible, Rachel promised to get a smaller one. She added, "You can also download the Bible on your phone."

Ruth preferred that; no one would know that she had the Bible.

"But I'll still get a physical one for you." Rachel promised. "You should have it."

Ruth shrugged.

"Bring your phone, I can download it for you." Rachel said and held her hand out.

"I'll do it myself." Ruth said. She wouldn't want Rachel to see the nude pictures on her phone.

Rachel spoke again. "There are lots of stuff on the Play Store. I need to show you the right Bible App to download."

Ruth held her phone in her hand, asked Rachel to show her the right Bible App, and she downloaded it immediately.

Rachel showed her how to use it, and Ruth thanked her.

While Rachel and her assistant attended to some things, Ruth brought out her camera, drew near the transparent jewelry display shelf in a corner, and took a picture of the jewelries in it.

When Rachel saw what Ruth was doing, she thanked her.

She came to Ruth and Ruth turned the camera to her so she could see the picture taken. It was good and very clear.

"I like it."

"You can post it on Instagram, it would look great." Ruth told her as she prepared to take another picture.

"I definitely will."

Ruth took some pictures, and then asked Rachel to come and stand by the shelf. Rachel did.

"No, there." Ruth pointed.

Rachel moved and then posed.

"Lean forward a little ... tilt your chin down ... more ... okay ... turn your body slightly to this side."

Click.

Ruth took about eight pictures and promised that she'd send them to Rachel after editing.

Just then, Linda called to let Ruth know that she'd be late in coming home.

*Oh, good!* "How was the meeting?"

"Great! I have good news. I'll tell you all about it when I get home. I'm still there."

"Alright. Take your time." Ruth said.

"Are you back at home?" Linda wanted to know.

"No, not yet."

About fifteen minutes to six, Ruth, Rachel, and her assistant left the store and went inside the church hall.

Ruth looked around—the walls were white. She noticed that the rug which covered the floor of the hall matched the crimson red padded single chairs that filled it. There were several windows but they were closed, and she could feel the air conditioner working. Musical instruments—

complete with microphones were on a side in front. Also in front by the altar were a projector and a large banner that denoted the vision of the church. A glass pulpit was on the altar.

Some people were already in the hall, and more people were arriving. The pastor, his wife, and some people entered the hall and went to some seats in front.

Rachel asked her to put her phone on silent so it would not start ringing during service, and she did.

As she sat beside Rachel, she felt a little uneasy and out of place. She never thought that this could happen to her. *I am now a Christian!* She almost couldn't believe it. When was the last time that she went to church?

The service started promptly with opening prayer and everyone stood. This was followed by praise and worship. The songs were projected on the screen, and as the congregation of about one hundred adults sang, clapped, and danced, Ruth glanced around, looking at them.

She didn't know any of the songs, they were not even her kind of songs. Hmm, some things would have to change in her life. She didn't know how, but she had been told that God would help her. *Well, we shall see.*

For the Bible study session, the congregation was divided into groups, and she and Rachel were together in a group. The topic was *Identity in* Christ.

Ruth's mind kept wandering as she thought of different things. But when she eventually focused and listened, she learned a lot. Afterward, everyone came together to hear the pastor preach.

The service ended around eight and they left the hall. Ruth offered to drop off Rachel at home, and when Rachel asked if she'd come in to greet their parents, she declined.

Rachel got down in front of the house, said goodnight, and Ruth drove away immediately.

On the way home, she was thinking about some of the things that she learned in the Bible study. One was about the fact that she had become a new person; the old life must be gone and a new life must begin. As she continued thinking, she felt like she had just stepped into a brand-new life.

Hmm. Linda was her major concern. She didn't care much about the other people in her life.

And where would she tell Linda that she was coming from at this time? She glanced at the clock on the dashboard, it was nine-ten. She thought about it and came up with a plan. If she met Linda at home, she would stay in the living room to work until she was sure Linda had slept. However, if she got home before Linda, she would go to bed as soon as possible to avoid intimacy with her. Besides, she was tired both in body and mind.

At home, there was no sign of Linda. She ate and showered. Just as she was about to head for the bedroom, she heard sounds at the door. She looked at the wall clock, it was ten-thirty-three. The door was unlocked and Linda entered the living room.

Hmm, she would have to go with the second plan—stay in the living room until Linda was asleep, Ruth told herself.

They greeted and Linda began to tell her about her day. Ruth had left food for Linda, and as Linda ate, she continued talking excitedly. An actress became unable to play her role in a movie due to an injury. A casting director had submitted Linda's name as a replacement, and now, the role had been given to her. The shooting for the movie would take two to three months and she would be going with the others to the shooting location next week.

"That's awesome!" Ruth commented, knowing how much this meant to Linda. Linda had been trying for some time to get another movie role.

Ruth was supposed to talk about her day too, and when it was her turn, she simply said that she had series of meetings. Linda would have asked for details, but still being excited about her news, she didn't bother to ask Ruth.

When it was time to go to bed, Ruth told Linda to go ahead without her as she had some work to do.

"Okay. Don't be late." Linda said.

Ruth went to her work table, sat, and opened her laptop while Linda went to the bedroom.

For some minutes however, all she could do was stare at the screen blankly. She eventually focused and was able to do some work. When she got up about two hours later and entered the bedroom, she found Linda asleep, snoring softly. She got in bed beside Linda and slept without praying.

The next day, the pastor's wife sent a message to her, to know what time she could call.

Ruth was at home alone and when she responded that she was available, Pastor Ida called and encouraged her to stand for God.

"Don't let anyone confuse you, you have made the right decision. If you have any question or concern, don't hesitate to let me know."

She prayed for Ruth and Ruth thanked her for calling.

Afterward, Ruth opened the Bible App on her phone to the book of John, and began to read Chapter one. It seemed like a story to her, but somehow, she found it interesting.

In bed at night, she decided to turn to Linda. She couldn't be giving Linda excuses every day. Besides, she needed the intimacy, she told herself.

In the afternoon of the next day, Thursday, Ruth was at home alone eating lunch when her older sister called. The woman wanted Ruth to come to her office to take some pictures for her, and they fixed a convenient time. While talking, Ruth mentioned that she took Rachel's pictures just two days ago.

When the call ended, Ruth spoke aloud, "I need to work on Rachel's pictures today and send them to her."

About a minute after, she received a call from Rachel.

"Talk of the devil and the devil appears." Ruth said and chuckled.

"No, talk of an angel and the angel appears."

"An angel? Why did you say that?" Ruth wanted to know.

"First of all, if you're referring to my unexpected call, I'm not a devil, I'm a child of God. And secondly, as Christians, we should watch what we say."

"But it's a common phrase."

"Yes, I know, but as Christians, we are ruled by God's laws, and we should not say things that can invite the devil." Rachel explained. "Were you talking about me with someone?"

Ruth told her that she had just talked about editing her pictures so that she could forward them to her.

They exchanged pleasantries and then Rachel told her that she'd need to be in church on Sunday morning for service.

"Church on Sunday morning?! Ahh!" Ruth complained. "I usually sleep in on Sunday mornings."

Rachel began to encourage her and she eventually agreed.

"Do you have appropriate clothes for church?" Rachel asked.

"Like what?"

"Something decent."

Ruth took a deep breath. "I don't know. I'll have to check. I should be able to find something though. What time will the service start?"

"It's nine to twelve."

Ruth groaned.

"It's for just about three hours. But, even if it's longer, you'll enjoy the service and before you know it, it's over." Rachel said by way of encouragement.

Ruth promised to be there. "What time are you likely to get there yourself?"

"Eight."

Ruth was surprised. *Does Rachel sleep at all?* "Eight?! Why?"

"Because I'm a worker in the church. I'm in prayer department. Workers are expected to get to church early." Rachel explained.

"Okay, but how will I see you when I get there?"

"Text me when you arrive." Rachel said.

After the call and lunch, Ruth went to her room and, checking her clothes in the closet, she realized that they were not appropriate for church. Most of them were men's clothes, and the female clothes were either too short or revealed too much cleavage or thigh. She might have to wear one of Linda's clothes.

She suddenly remembered that she had kept two clothes she didn't want in an under-the-bed storage box. Bending down, she pulled out the box and checked the clothes—a multicolored kaftan and a red gown with sleeves. Some people had given them to her but she had never worn them. Deciding she'd wear the gown, she wanted to put it on the bed. But, knowing that if Linda saw it, she would want to know why she'd want to wear it, she returned it into the box and pushed the box back under the bed.

Back in the living room, she sat at her work table, opened her laptop, and began to work on Rachel's pictures.

She was still working on them when Linda arrived. They greeted and Linda came over to give her a peck.

Her eyes went to the picture on the laptop. "Is that not your sister?" She had not met Rachel but had seen some of her pictures with Ruth.

"Yes."

"Where's this? I didn't know you saw her recently," Linda commented.

"Yes, I did. The pictures were taken in her store." Ruth answered, and to prevent Linda from asking further questions about why and when she saw Rachel, she quickly changed the line of discussion.

When she was through with the pictures, she e-mailed them to Rachel.

Later in the bedroom, she told Linda that she'd be attending a meeting on Sunday morning and she'd have to wear a dress.

"What meeting is that?"

"It's a kind of a family meeting."

"Which dress do you have in mind?"

Ruth brought out the red gown and wore it. "What do you think?"

Linda shrugged and said it was okay.

That Sunday morning, Ruth got ready and after light breakfast, left for church, with her camera in a bag. The white gate of the church was open, and the gate guard checked each car before allowing it to pass.

After the security check, Ruth drove inside the compound and parked her car on a side of the parking lot as directed by a male uniformed usher. Bringing out her phone, she sent a text to Rachel to inform her that she had arrived in church. She knew that the service had started as she could hear music. She checked the time on her phone and it was nine-eleven. Carrying her camera bag, she alighted from the car, and as she walked toward the church hall, she pressed the lock button on the car key to lock the car doors.

Five female ushers were standing by the entrance of the hall, holding some pamphlets and she walked toward them.

Rachel appeared with a broad smile and waited for Ruth at the entrance.

When Ruth got there, one of the ushers stepped forward, welcomed her to church, and gave her one of the pamphlets in her hand.

Rachel hugged Ruth in greeting, obviously happy to see her. She told the ushers that she had reserved a seat for Ruth, and then she led Ruth inside the hall to their seats.

Putting the camera bag down on the floor by her feet, Ruth glanced around. The choristers who were adorned in red and green robes were on a side, singing, and Pastor Joel and his wife were at their place in front with some other ministers.

The choir members began another song which Ruth realized that they sang when she attended the Bible study on Tuesday. With the lyrics on the projector, she was able to sing along.

The service continued, and when newcomers were being recognized, Rachel asked her to stand but she refused to.

Soon, it was time for the sermon and Pastor Joel got on the altar with his Bible in his hand. In his message, he talked about the importance of confessing God's words.

"You have to realize that God sees and hears you. Use your mouth to say what God has said in His word."

The message was powerful and when he made a call for those who wished to make new spiritual commitment to Jesus to come forward to the altar, Ruth found herself leaving her seat. Four other people joined her at the altar and the pastor prayed for them. Afterward, the five people who responded to the call were led to a side of the hall by a woman. When the service ended, the woman who introduced herself as the pastor in charge of New Believer's

Class, encouraged them, and collected their names and phone numbers.

Rachel was waiting for Ruth and when Ruth came to her, she said that Pastor Joel and his wife would like to see Ruth. Some church members came to Rachel and when she told them that Ruth was her sister and had just become a Christian, they greeted Ruth warmly.

She Who Has a Man | Taiwo Iredele Odubiyi

# CHAPTER 6

Rachel and Ruth exited the hall, and went to Pastor Joel's office. His wife was there, and it was obvious that they were happy Ruth came to church and also responded to the altar call. They told her that she'd need to join the New Believer's Class, which would hold every Sunday morning for eight weeks, and that they would also assign two female members to disciple her.

Ruth did not really understand what they meant by the word 'disciple', but from what they were saying, she gathered that it meant the women were to help her grow and become established in her Christian faith.

Summoning the two women, Pastor Joel introduced them to Ruth, and told Ruth that the women would be in touch with her soon.

"They will need your phone number and address." Pastor Joel added.

"We already have the information, sir." One of the women said.

"Oh good." Pastor Joel nodded and then told Ruth to expect to see them before the week ended.

*They will come to my house? I've not told Linda that I've been coming to church! What will Linda say if she sees them in the house?* It was at that point that Ruth realized that she had not thought of Linda since she got to church in the morning.

The two women left and the pastors prayed for Ruth.

When they asked if she had any concern, she confessed that she didn't know how she would handle Linda.

"Have you told her that you're now born again?" Pastor Ida asked.

Ruth shook her head. "No."

"So, where did you tell her you were going this morning?"

"I told her that I was going to some sort of a family meeting."

"So, you lied?"

"Yes." She admitted.

"Now that you're a Christian, you have to do things God's way. A Christian is not supposed to tell lies."

Ruth nodded in understanding.

"There's what is known as a white lie, but a white lie is still a lie, and it's a sin before God."

As Pastor Ida showed her some scriptures to confirm her words, Ruth realized that lying was another thing that God would have to deliver her from as she lied a lot.

Pastor Joel added, "Besides, God does not want us to be ashamed of Him. Let your friends and families know that you're now a new person."

"Yes, sir." Ruth said.

Of course, the pastors were right. She would have to let Linda know that she had changed, but how? And how would Linda take it? Knowing that Linda would be leaving on Tuesday for the shooting location and would be away for some time, she told herself that she still had time to make a decision and come up with a plan.

When they left the pastor's office, Rachel took Ruth to the church bookshop where she bought some things for Ruth—a small Bible, a mini book on faith, two highlighters, and a notebook to take notes during church service and when studying the Bible.

When they were walking toward Ruth's car, Rachel said, "Daddy and Mommy need to know that you're now a Christian. They need to know that I've been seeing you. When will you tell them?"

"Yes, I'll tell them but not now." Ruth answered.

In her car on the way home, Ruth was thinking about what was happening in her life. God was definitely working on her heart.

And then, her mind went to Linda. She couldn't be intimate with Linda tonight even though she'd want to. It would be wrong to do that and God would not be happy with her.

Then she asked aloud, "But how am I going to get through this situation?"

She sighed. God would have to deliver her, somehow.

Shortly after she got home, she received a chat on WhatsApp from one of the two women. The woman wanted to know when she could visit Ruth. But Ruth did not respond; she'd need to think about it.

That night, when she told Linda again that she was tired, Linda was concerned and asked her to see a doctor.

"No, there's no need. I'll be fine."

"But I'm traveling on Tuesday and you'll be at home alone! You need to do something."

"No, I'll be fine." She assured Linda.

When she remembered that she had not replied the message of the woman assigned to follow her up, she took her phone and told her on WhatsApp that she'd be available on Wednesday or Thursday morning if the woman could make it.

Monday was busy for Linda. Because she would have to meet the movie crew and cast at an agreed location on Tuesday, she had to make some calls and see some people.

On Tuesday, Ruth drove her to the place around noon and returned home.

On Wednesday morning, around eleven, the two women visited Ruth. They taught her how to pray, prayed for her, and encouraged her to join the New Believers Class. Then they left.

Afterward, she drove to Rachel's store, and together, they went to some stores where she bought some female clothes that were appropriate for church.

In church on Sunday morning, Ruth joined the New Believer's Class which held in a room at eight-thirty, and when it ended at nine, everyone in the class went to the main church hall for service.

When the service ended, she offered to take Rachel home.

"I hope there's food to eat at home."

"I'm not sure but I can ask Mom. You'll come inside the house?" Rachel asked, happy.

"Yes."

"I can call Mom and tell her that you're coming home with me, and that you'd like to eat."

"Okay." Ruth responded. Then she laughed. "I'm sure she will want to know why we're coming home together."

Rachel chuckled and took her phone to make the call.

Ruth stopped her. "Better still, just tell her that a church member is coming home with you, and would like to eat. Let it be a surprise."

They laughed.

Rachel made the call and went for her departmental meeting which would last about forty minutes. While Ruth waited for her, she interacted with some church members.

When Rachel was ready, she called Ruth. As they walked toward Ruth's car, Rachel called her mother to know if food was ready, and her mother said yes.

"Okay, we'll be there soon."

The drive took about twenty five minutes. They alighted from the car and went inside the house.

Rachel opened the front door and stepped inside the living room, followed by Ruth.

Their parents were there and they greeted them. They were surprised but happy to see Ruth. As Ruth responded to their greetings, they realized that something about her was different, but they couldn't figure it out.

Their mother turned her attention to Rachel. "Where's your church member that you said would like to eat?"

"This is the person." Rachel pointed at Ruth.

Ruth smiled while their parents looked at them in confusion.

Then their mother took a closer look at Ruth and noticed the way she was dressed. What was going on?

"What do you mean by church member?" Their mother asked.

Smiling, Rachel looked at Ruth. "That question is for you."

Putting her bag down on the nearest seat, Ruth removed her shoes, and said, "I know. I'm hungry, and I need to get my food first."

"Everything is on the table." Their mother said and pointed at the table. "We haven't eaten too, so we'll just eat together."

Rachel removed her shoes, put her handbag and Bible down, and followed Ruth to the table.

Their parents joined them. Rachel got bottles of water from the refrigerator, and after blessing the food, Ruth and Rachel served their food.

Their mother got food for their father, sat down, and looked from Rachel to Ruth.

"What about your own food?" Rachel asked her.

"I'd like to hear what Ruth has to say first." She answered. Looking at Ruth, she asked, "Where did you meet?"

"I'm now a Christian." Ruth said simply.

Their mother looked from her to Rachel and asked, "Is that true?"

"Yes, Mommy." Rachel answered, smiling broadly.

"Hallelujah!" She shouted.

"I'm sure that you now see how great Jesus is," Rachel said.

"Yes," Their mother answered.

When they finished eating, Rachel began to talk to her parents about Jesus, and when she asked if they were willing to give their lives to Jesus, her mother said yes. Her father didn't seem to be interested.

As Rachel prayed for her, Ruth looked at them in amazement. *Is this how God works?!*

When their mother said she'd come to church the following Sunday with Rachel, Ruth promised to come early enough to pick them up.

She eventually left her parents' house around six in the evening and at home, she deleted the nude pictures and pornographic videos on her phone and laptop. She no longer needed them.

She had a job on Tuesday afternoon, and as soon as she could leave, she did and went to church for service. She got there late; the Bible study had started and she joined the appropriate class.

On Thursday evening, she was back in church for prayer service.

Over the next few weeks, Ruth found herself growing spiritually. Since Linda was not around, she had some time to herself which she spent reading the Bible, talking to God, and going to church. She also watched Christian movies.

The two women from the church had been coming regularly to disciple her. They made her know what it meant to be a Christian, and how a Christian should think, talk, act, and live. They taught her how to pray and study the Bible. They also taught her some songs, recommended some Christian books to her, and encouraged her to create time to listen to their pastors' teachings on YouTube or the church's website as they would strengthen her.

And in the New Believers Class in church, she was learning a lot. The teachers had taught the class about the Holy Spirit, how to be led by the Holy Spirit, and the importance of the resurrection of Jesus, among other topics. She was water baptized and when the teachers ministered Holy Spirit baptism to her, she spoke in tongues.

Rachel had also been helpful, giving her books to read, and answering her questions. The questions she couldn't answer were referred to the pastor's wife.

All the things that Pastor Joel had been saying and which she'd heard about Christianity before she encountered God were now making sense to her. Her heart had definitely changed.

Her attitude had changed toward the things of God and how she spent her time. She had bought a bigger Bible when she realized that the small one did not serve much purpose for her, and she now called Pastor Joel and Pastor Ida 'Daddy and Mommy'.

Her attitude had also changed toward money, and she now paid tithe on her earnings.

She had been added to the church's Singles group on WhatsApp. She realized that the singles had fellowship in church every Friday evening at seven and she planned to attend soon.

On the first Monday of July, she bought more female clothes, and much later at home, she sat in her living room to read the Bible. She got to Matthew chapter five, and as she read verses twenty nine and thirty, the words seemed to pierce her heart. She decided to check the Amplified version for better understanding and read the words out.

*If your right eye makes you stumble and leads you to sin, tear it out and throw it away [that is, remove yourself from the source of temptation]; for it is better for you to lose one of the parts of your body, than for your whole body to be thrown into hell. If your right hand makes you stumble and leads you to sin, cut it off and throw it away [that is, remove yourself from the source of temptation]; for it is better for you to lose one of the parts of your body than for your whole body to go into hell.*

It was now very clear to her that God wanted her to end her relationship with Linda quickly, thereby cutting the string that tied her to the past. She would have to lose Linda than disobey God and lose God's favor and heaven.

As she continued reading the Bible, another thing became very clear to her—following Jesus meant that she must deny herself. She knew it would not be easy but she also knew that whatever she might have to give up would be nothing compared to all that Jesus did for her.

When she finished reading the chapter, she put the Bible down and began to think of how she would tell Linda when she returned that she was now a Christian and would have to end their relationship. Linda had been away for about a month now. They talked almost every day and from what Linda said yesterday, she would return home by the end of July or early August.

Ruth thought of different ways to break the news to Linda, but there was really no easy way to do it.

She prayed. "Lord, help me, I can't do this on my own."

She had two jobs the next day—one in the morning and the other in the afternoon—and when she was through, she went to church for Bible study. When the service ended, she went with her sister to Pastor Joel to tell him that she had a concern. When she said that she would like to see him, he asked her to come on Friday afternoon.

She was there on Friday, and the pastor's PA said that she could go into the pastor's office.

Pastor Ida was in the office with her husband and after greeting them, Ruth began to talk about her concern.

She went on. "Daddy, I really don't know how I will tell Linda. She's presently not around, but she will be back soon."

They could see that she was really troubled. After counseling her, they summoned Rachel, and suggested that Rachel and another church member, preferably a male, should be in the house with Ruth on the day that Linda would return to give her support.

"But ... is it not possible for us to convert her?" Ruth asked.

The pastors smiled while Rachel looked on with concern and prayed under her breath that God would strengthen Ruth.

Pastor Joel shook his head as he answered, "No human being can convert another person, only God can. We will try to reach out to her, though."

Pastor Ida nodded in agreement.

He went on. "However, getting her saved is one thing while your relationship with her is a different thing. Whether she's saved on not, you have to end your relationship with her."

Pastor Ida nodded again.

Ruth took a deep breath. "I know ... but ... she's going to be upset." She predicted.

"It's understandable, but it cannot be helped." Pastor Ida commented.

Pastor Joel asked, "Have you been intimate with her since the day you gave your life to Jesus?"

Ruth was tempted to lie but she did not. She knew she must please God.

She nodded. "Yes, twice. We sleep in the same room."

They told her that she would have to stop.

"Do you have only a room?" Pastor Ida asked.

"No, the second one is supposed to be for her, but since she shares my room, the other room has been for visitors and also serves as my photo studio." She said.

"She will need to leave your room immediately." Pastor Joel instructed. "If she has another house to move to, that would be better. If not, you can give her some time to find a place and move out. But, until then, there should be no more intimacy with her. The relationship should be terminated immediately. I hope you understand?"

"Yes, Daddy."

"The best thing would be for her to leave immediately." Pastor Ida said. "She has friends and some family members, I'm sure."

Ruth nodded to confirm.

Pastor Ida went on. "This is because she's not an ordinary friend, you've had a relationship with her. It's like a lady in an ungodly relationship with a man. She needs to separate herself if she would do the right thing. To continue to live together will not work."

Patiently, they answered her questions and then prayed for her.

When she left, she entered the church and while she waited for the singles fellowship to start, she used her phone.

Soon, members of the fellowship began to arrive. Rachel and her assistant also entered the hall, and at the appropriate time, the fellowship began. Greatly blessed,

Ruth decided she would attend the fellowship as much as possible so that she could learn about Christian relationship.

After service on Sunday, Rachel and their mother, who had been coming to church, decided to go home with Ruth to spend the day with her. On the way, Ruth stopped at a restaurant to buy food that they would eat at her house. In her apartment, they blessed the food and as they ate, they talked.

Ruth had always thought that her mother did not love her much because she was very strict with her. There had always been tension in her relationship with her mother, but as they discussed and laughed, she realized that she had been wrong. Her mother's strictness stemmed from love, and she had only been trying to make Ruth become a good woman. She made up her mind to be closer to her mother.

When they were ready to leave around seven in the evening, Ruth took her car keys to drop them off.

On the first day of August, a Saturday, Linda called Ruth and told her that she would be coming back on Sunday, August 9.

Immediately after the call, Ruth sent a message to the pastor's wife and Rachel, informing them of the date.

Within a minute, Pastor Ida replied.

*Ok. The Lord is in control. See me after service tomorrow.*

Afterward, Ruth prayed that God would strengthen her to do the right thing.

In church the next day, she attended the New Believers Class as she had been doing for the past eight weeks. The class that morning was the last one for her, and at the end, the pastor in charge encouraged the members to join departments and become church workers. Ruth had already decided to join the ushering department and she told the pastor so.

The main church service started promptly and when it ended, Ruth and Rachel went to Pastor Ida who took them to Pastor Joel. When they explained to him that Linda was expected back next Sunday, he called one of the men in the church, Kenneth, and told him that he and Rachel would go to Ruth's house after church service the following Sunday.

That week was particularly busy for Ruth as she had jobs to do on Wednesday, Thursday, and Friday. The one on Friday would be a photoshoot for a popular female model. She couldn't attend prayer meeting on Thursday as she needed to prepare for the photoshoot. She also contacted someone to go with her to the location of the photoshoot to assist her.

On Friday, she loaded her car with her equipment, picked up her assistant, and headed to the location. Everyone, including the hair stylist and makeup artist came on time. They went over what to do, and then it was time to start.

The model—a tall beautiful lady—changed her clothes, had her hair and makeup done, and then it was time to start. With some music playing in the background, Ruth clicked away, taking pictures from different angles, and telling the model what to do. After some time, the first segment was over and while the model got ready for the second session, Ruth rearranged the set and got her equipment ready. She and her assistant also got something to drink. Soon, they began the next series of shots, and when they finished, they packed up and left.

Ruth dropped off her assistant and back at home, she ate, and then dragged her tired body to the bathroom to have a shower. Later in bed, she began to pray and speak in tongues. Sunday would definitely bring about more changes in her life.

## CHAPTER 7

After service on Sunday afternoon, Rachel and Kenneth—the male church member assigned by Pastor Joel—went home with Ruth. They prayed that Linda would not cause any problem and that she would become a Christian soon. Afterward, they ate lunch.

At about two-twenty, Linda called Ruth to say that one of the crew members would bring her home, and that they were on the way.

Soon, Linda arrived. She wasn't surprised to see visitors in the living room as the house doubled as a photo studio. What surprised her was that Ruth did not embrace her as she usually did. Ruth only got up and greeted her, but did not come close. Did Ruth not miss her?

Linda greeted everyone and went inside the bedroom. Another surprise—Ruth did not follow her.

When she came out, Ruth asked if she would eat and when she said yes, Ruth served her food.

As Linda ate, she gave the visitors a closer look and recognized Rachel. What was she doing here?

After eating, she took her dishes to the kitchen, washed them, and returned to the living room.

With her heart pounding, Ruth called her and said, "Please sit down."

Linda looked at her face. What was going on? Did something happen? And who was the man with Rachel? Had they come to break some bad news to her?

Then her eyes went to one of the books on the table in front of Ruth, and saw what was written on the hard cover—Holy Bible.

*Holy Bible*? Something was very wrong, Linda thought with a frown.

She sat down and looked at Ruth. There was sorrow in Ruth's eyes which she didn't understand.

Ruth went on. "This is Rachel, my sister."

*Yes, I already figured that out. What I'd like to know is what brought her here*, Linda thought.

"Hello," Rachel smiled at Linda.

Linda simply nodded.

"And this is Brother Kenneth."

Linda looked at him.

"Hello,"

Linda ignored Kenneth's greeting and returned her gaze to Ruth.

Ruth continued. "I have to tell you something."

Linda's frown deepened.

"I am now a Christian."

The words hung in the air for some seconds as Linda wondered if she'd heard correctly.

"A what?!" She couldn't have heard right, surely. It wasn't possible!

"I'm now a Christian." Ruth repeated. "I've been going to church."

Linda glared at her in disbelief. "Why?"

"I now know the truth. Jesus has saved me." Ruth added as she fought back tears.

Linda did not talk. She didn't even understand what Ruth was saying. What truth? Her expression showed that she was struggling to believe Ruth's words. But the look on Ruth's face said she was serious.

Summoning up courage, Ruth spoke again, "I'm sorry but I will ... we will have to end our relationship."

Shocked, Linda felt that she stopped breathing for some seconds. Then she took a breath to speak. "You're joking, right?"

Ruth wept silently. *Lord, help me*. She didn't like to hurt Linda's feelings.

"You're serious?!" Linda could hardly get the words out. *What's happening?*

Ruth nodded. "Yes, I am."

Linda still couldn't believe it. How was that even possible? Ruth did not like Christians; she could not stand them and anything about Christianity made her skin crawl.

So, how could this happen? Had she been hypnotized? Was she under some form of spell?

"Really?" She forced herself to ask.

Ruth nodded. "Yes."

Linda felt like getting up and walking away, but there were questions she had to ask, and now.

She got up. "We need to talk. Can we go inside the room?"

As Ruth made to get up, Kenneth called her, to stop her.

"It's okay. It's fine." Ruth told him.

Linda gave Kenneth a bad look, turned, and walked toward the room.

Ruth followed her.

In the room, Ruth closed the door and said, "I'm sorry, Linda."

She hoped Linda would understand. But how could she expect Linda to, when she didn't fully understand herself?

"Ruth, did they do something to you? Are you being blackmailed?" Linda asked, looking perplexed.

"No." Ruth answered. "Let me explain what happened."

"Okay, I'm listening." Linda said and sat down.

Ruth remained standing. "Remember I told you some time ago that I had a dream,"

"Dream? Yes," *What has that got to do with this?* Linda wondered.

Ruth revealed what she saw in the dream and the other dreams.

When she stopped, Linda said, "So, all this is because of the dreams you had?"

"No, it's about Jesus. He loves you too, Linda. He's waiting for you to come to Him -"

Linda stopped her. "Don't! Don't try to preach to me!"

Ruth stopped and took a deep breath.

Linda spoke again. "So, what will happen to us?"

"I'm now a Christian, I have to glorify God." Even though her voice was full of regret, Ruth was sure of what she was doing.

She added, "We can only be friends." *How can I be ordinary friends with her? How can we go from lovers to friends? How's that possible*? She had doubts, but this was not a time to think about that.

"But you said you would not leave me. You promised me." Linda reminded her of her promise.

"Yes, I did, and I kept my promise. I'm taking this step because I now realize that the relationship is wrong."

"Don't do this to us," Linda said desperately.

Then she touched Ruth.

"No, Linda." Ruth stepped back. "Don't make this difficult for us, please."

Linda dropped her hand, took a deep breath and said under her breath, *this is crazy*.

Then she asked, "Do you want me to move out?"

"You may have to ... but you can stay until you find another place. I'm sorry." Ruth said.

"One week? One month? Two months?"

"As soon as you find another place. I'm sure you will find somewhere soon."

Linda's mouth turned into a sad smile. "I can see that you've thought of everything."

"I'm sorry, Linda."

When Linda realized that there was nothing left to say, she left the room angrily, went inside the second room, and locked the door.

Ruth returned to the living room.

"What did she say?" Rachel asked her.

Ruth told them.

They were still talking when Linda came out. She entered the room she shared with Ruth and closed the door. Within two minutes, the door opened again and she emerged, carrying a handbag. She headed for the door.

"Where are you going?" Ruth asked her, concerned.

"Out." She said at the door.

"Linda, I'm sorry -"

But Linda raised a hand in her direction to say that she didn't want to hear whatever she had to say. And with that, she left.

Rachel offered to stay with Ruth because they didn't know what Linda might do.

Ruth shook her head. "She can't do anything. She won't harm me. She's not that kind of a person."

"You can't be sure about that. You have just ended your relationship." Rachel said.

Kenneth added, "Don't underestimate her. An angry person can do anything. Besides, don't forget that she's not a Christian. Someone who is not a Christian can do anything."

Ruth remembered what she watched on TV about a man's ex who set his house on fire. *Hmm, Rachel and Brother Kenneth are right.*

"That's true." She had to admit.

They also advised that she'd need to change the lock of the door as soon as Linda moved out of the house since Linda had a key.

At about six, Rachel went into the kitchen to see what she could cook. They ate and shortly after, Kenneth left.

Around nine in the evening, one of Ruth's female friends called her and said Linda had just finished speaking with her. "Is what she told me true?"

"What did she tell you?"

"She said you told her that you're now a Christian. I told her it's not possible and that you must have said that as an excuse. What exactly happened, Ruth? Is there another person?"

"No." Ruth answered, then thought about her answer and decided to change it. "Well, yes."

"Who? Have you just met her?"

"Yes, but it's not her, it's Him."

"Him? You, Ruth?" Surprise was obvious in the lady's voice.

"Yes."

"Wow! Interesting! That's a first, right?"

"Yes." Ruth answered.

"If that's the case, why didn't you tell Linda the truth? Why did you lie to her? Who is this man anyway? Does he have a name?"

"Yes, His name is Jesus."

"Jesus?! Are you sure you're okay, Ruth?"

When Ruth did not respond, she spoke again, "Are you in some kind of danger? If yes, you don't need to say a word, just say 'umm hmm', and I'll get help for you."

"There's no problem." Ruth said and explained how she became a Christian.

The lady began to argue with Ruth and when Ruth told her that she needed Jesus, she got angry and ended the call.

Linda returned to the house around midnight, and when she found Rachel sleeping in the living room, she went to the guest room to sleep.

In the evening of the next day, Linda moved out, taking all the things she brought into the apartment. She also removed her photographs from Ruth's room.

In bed that night, Ruth cried. For about two months, she had been sleeping alone in bed because Linda traveled, but now, she was sleeping alone because Linda was out of her life. What next?

Did this mean no intimacy until she got married to a man? A man? Who would that be? When would that be? How would it be? She had not even been attracted to a man!

And where was he? How would she find him?! To find a man was one thing, and to find a man who would marry her was another thing. And how would she cope until then? How would she cope with being with a man?!

Early morning sunlight had filtered through the curtains when she woke up on Tuesday. Turning to lay on her right side, her mind went to all that happened in the last two days—how Linda moved out. What was Linda thinking about her now? Where did she move to?

Taking her phone, she sent a text to Linda to say that she did not mean to hurt her, but there was no response.

When she went to church on Friday evening for singles' meeting, she looked at the men who were around. She had come to know some of them and they were nice. She got along well with them, but she was not attracted to any of them. *Will I ever be attracted to one of their kind?* She wondered.

Looking at one of the men, she imagined being held by him, and she shook her head. *This is going to be hard.*

Realizing that the thought was wrong, she sighed, corrected herself, and prayed under her breath, "No, it will not be hard for me in Jesus' name. Holy Spirit, help me, make it easy for me!"

At that time, her mind went to Linda. She had been trying hard not to think of Linda, but now, she wondered where she was and what she was doing.

Soon, the fellowship started and she focused on the service.

In bed at home much later, she sent a message to Linda and found that Linda had blocked her e-mail to her and phone.

Ruth felt bad. Giving up and going back to her old way of life seemed easier than having to deal with all these issues. She was tempted to give up, look for Linda and apologise, but she knew she should not.

She prayed instead, "Lord, strengthen me!"

She had indeed lost Linda. She had also lost some of her friends and as she thought about this, the Holy Spirit made her remember that she had gained new friends.

*That's true*, she nodded thoughtfully and allowed herself to think of some of her new friends. But still, she thought of the past.

In church on Sunday, she felt better. However, on Monday morning, she woke up with a heavy heart.

After praying briefly, she decided to go out. She needed to talk to someone. She didn't have any place in mind, and she headed to Rachel's place.

Fortunately for her, Rachel was not busy.

"Have you had breakfast?"

"No." Ruth answered.

"I've not eaten as well." Rachel said. "Let's go and find something to eat."

They went to a restaurant and as they ate, they talked. When Ruth told her some of her concerns, Rachel asked her to see the pastors.

They finished eating, returned to the church, and went in the direction of Pastor Ida's office. The woman was not around and they decided to see Pastor Joel.

He asked about Linda and she answered that she had not heard from Linda since she moved out of her house.

She told the pastor some of her concerns and asked different questions.

She went on. "Another question, will I find a man who would marry me in spite of my story?"

Patiently, he answered her questions and assured her that nothing was too hard or impossible for God to do, and that God would give her the right man to marry if she allowed Him to lead her.

"God will give you a man who is reliable and caring—a true child of God." He added.

Ruth nodded. She had been observing some of the men in church and found that they were reliable, caring, and trustworthy. Before now, some of the men she knew were lousy and two-faced. Even her father cheated on her mother. But now, she knew that good men existed, and that she could be in good hands.

He prayed for her, and by the time she was leaving, she was feeling better and assured of a wonderful future.

On her way home, while speaking in tongues, her mind went to her male clothes and shoes, and she knew that it was time for her to give them all out. At home, she went inside her room, threw open her closet, and began to bring them out—clothes, shoes, belt, ties. Looking at the huge pile on the floor of her room, she called Rachel.

"I'm wondering if I should bring them to church."

"Yes, please do. They will be useful to some men." Rachel said.

"That's what I thought. Okay, I'll bring them tomorrow." She said.

After the call, she wondered, *what else do I need to do?*

She thought about her hair and decided to grow it a little. She'd still like a low cut, but it would have to be in a feminine way. Or better still, make it curly. She went online to see some pictures that would give her an idea of what to do.

On Tuesday afternoon, she put the items in her car, went to church, and handed them over to Pastor Joel's PA as Pastor Ida instructed her to do. Pastor Ida prayed for her for surrendering her life to Jesus, and afterward, she sat in the church hall to wait for Bible study.

The following day, she went to some stores to buy more female clothes.

She missed prayer service on Thursday because of a job, but attended Singles Fellowship on Friday.

In the morning of the last Sunday of October, as she dressed up for church, she remembered the past and smiled. Sunday morning was when she slept in or watched TV. But now, she was on her way to church. Her heart had truly changed.

The Holy Spirit had also been teaching her how to be the kind of woman that God wanted her to be—a God-fearing virtuous woman who is clothed with strength and dignity. She had also come to know some scriptures by heart. She was still a long way from the destination, but she knew that she was on the way and that gave her joy.

She went to church and soon, it was time for praise and worship, and the choir began to sing.

*Savior, Savior, Savior,*
*The one you saved has come to worship You.*

The song touched her heart and as she joined the congregation to sing it, tears ran down her face.

*Healer, Healer, Healer,*
*The one you healed has come to worship You.*

After the praise and worship session which lasted about twenty five minutes, they prayed, and the service continued.

When it was testimony time, four people went forward. As the first person gave his testimony, talking about God's goodness in his life, Ruth realized that she also had a testimony to share.

*Should I share it or keep quiet? How much of it should I share? What will the people who do not know my story say or think about me?*

As she considered these things, she felt that the prompting to talk was by the Holy Spirit. God wanted her to talk about what Jesus had done in her life. She got up, went forward, and joined the queue.

When it was her turn, she collected the microphone and asked the moderator, Pastor Zack, if she could sing a song.

"No, there's no time to sing." He told her.

"Pastor Zack," Pastor Joel called out from where he sat.

"Yes, sir," Pastor Zach turned to look at the senior pastor.

"Let her sing."

"Yes, sir."

Some people laughed, including Ruth.

She thanked the pastor and began to sing.

*You Did Not Wait For Me To Draw Nigh To You,*
*But You Clothed Yourself In Frail Humanity.*

*You Did Not Wait For Me To Cry Out To You,*
*But You Let Me Hear Your Voice Calling Me.*
*And I'm Forever Grateful, Lord, To You.*
*And I'm Forever Grateful For The Cross.*
*And I'm Forever Grateful To You,*
*That You Came To Seek And Save The Lost.*

Then she said, "That song is the summary of my testimony. God did not wait for me to look for Him, He looked for me, and saved me. While I was yet a sinner, Jesus died for me. When I was getting ready for church this morning, I remembered that Sunday morning was when I tried to relax. I woke up late and watched TV while having breakfast in bed, but now, I go to church, and I'm loving it."

People clapped.

"I've come to realize that everyone has a past, but some people's past may be more tainted. I belong to this group of people. Aside being a lesbian, I committed all manners of sins, and anything about God upset me. Because God knew that I would not listen to a preacher, He used some powerful dreams to get my attention. I contacted my sister, Rachel, and she led me to Daddy." She pointed in Pastor Joel's direction.

She went on. "I didn't want to listen to him, but there was a way that he talked that made me want to listen. He didn't condemn me, but patiently told me what the Bible says, and now I'm born again."

People clapped again.

"I give God all the glory." Then she turned and looked at Pastor Joel where he sat with his wife. "I also thank you, Daddy and Mommy."

It occurred to her to kneel down to appreciate the pastor. *Kneel down to appreciate him? In the presence of everyone?! Where did that voice come from?*

She wasn't used to doing such things, but sensing that it must be the voice of the Holy Spirit, she chose to obey. *Is Christianity not about pleasing God?*

She knelt down and repeated, "Thank you, Daddy."

Pastor Joel clapped and said, "Glory to God!"

"And thank you, Mommy."

Pastor Ida responded, "Praise God."

Ruth got up and went on. "I also thank my sister, Rachel, and all the people that God has been using for me."

Then she said Hallelujah to end her speech, and returned to her seat amidst claps. Pastor Zach prayed for all the people that gave testimonies, and handed over the microphone to another minister, a female.

One of the ushers came to Ruth and told her that Pastor Ida would like to see her after the service.

The female minister on the altar asked the congregation to stand to sing a hymn—the Comforter has come. Ruth didn't know it and she listened as the church sang the first verse and the chorus that were projected on the screen.

*O spread the tidings 'round, wherever man is found,*
*Wherever human hearts and human woes abound;*
*Let ev'ry Christian tongue proclaim the joyful sound:*
*The Comforter has come!*
*The Comforter has come, the Comforter has come,*
*The Holy Ghost from Heav'n, the Father's promise giv'n;*
*O spread the tidings 'round, wherever man is found?*
*The Comforter has come!*

Ruth found the hymn easy to learn and she joined the congregation in singing the remaining verses.

After the service, she went to see the pastor's wife who asked if she'd be attending the Singles Convention that would be coming up on Saturday, October 31.

"Yes, Ma. I may be a little late though because I have a job."

"Alright, no problem. Would you be willing to share your story at the event? People need to hear it." Pastor Ida said and then added, "It's possible that some of the invited people who will be present are going through such challenges or know some people who are. Hearing your testimony will encourage them to get the right help."

"Yes, Ma." Ruth said in agreement.

Alone at home later, Ruth realized that more people needed to know what God had done for her, and she decided to announce it on her social media platforms. Since she became a Christian on June 2, she posted only pictures and videos of her jobs. But now, it was time for God to be glorified.

A voice spoke to her – *why do you want to announce it? You're not even a strong Christian yet. Besides, if you fall back into sin after announcing it, you will be mocked. Don't announce it, be quiet about it.*

Ruth considered the words. *Hmm, what if I fall back?*

But another voice spoke to her and said – *you won't fall back if you follow the leading of the Holy Spirit. Why would you allow satan to take you back?*

"I won't go back in Jesus' name!" She prayed and decided to go ahead with her plan.

She had taken a picture of herself in church in the morning, and selecting the picture on her phone, she designed a beautiful frame for it and added a text:

*Born again and loving it!*

On Instagram, she posted it with the caption:

*Glory to God! Happy Sunday, everyone.*

She shared the designed frame and caption on Facebook and her WhatsApp status, and then used the designed frame as her WhatsApp display picture.

She posted the frame and the caption in the WhatsApp group chat of her university classmates and almost immediately, a male member commented.

*Born again? Ruth? The world must be coming to an end!*

Smiling, Ruth responded.
*Yes, I'm now born again, Jesus has saved me.*

Another male commented.
*I need to get out of here!*

Ruth responded.
*Come back here. Are you born again?*

People began to chat. Some of those who were Christians congratulated her while those who were not Christians cracked jokes about her confession.

About two hours after, Desmond called her. "I saw your post on Instagram. Is it true?"

Ruth laughed. "Yes, it is."

He was surprised. "You?"

"Yes, me."

"Tell me how it happened."

Ruth did.

"So, what about Linda?" Desmond couldn't help asking.

"It's over between us."

"Wow!" Desmond exclaimed. "How did she take it?"

"Not well."

Desmond laughed.

"Well, what about you? Are you born again?" She asked Desmond.

"Well, er... I think that I am."

Ruth told him that if he was truly born again, he would know, and she gave some evidences of a changed life.

Desmond wanted to know if her changed life would affect her profession in any way, and she said no.

She added, "It won't. It will make it better, if anything. Now, I have the Holy Spirit to guide me, to make me know what to do and what not to do, jobs to accept and the ones I shouldn't accept."

"So, what about my wedding? Does the arrangement for you to cover the ceremony still stand?"

Ruth laughed again. "Yes, sure."

## CHAPTER 8

That Sunday evening, Tokunbo checked WhatsApp, and when he saw Ruth's post and members' chats in the group, he was greatly surprised. He decided to send a message to her.

*I'm glad to know that you're now born again. I pray that the same power that raised Jesus from the dead, and which delivered me from my past, will uphold you, in Jesus' name.*

Ruth responded.

*Thank you, Tokunbo. How are you doing?*

*I'm doing well. I'm curious to know how you met the Lord, but if you don't want to share it, I'd understand.*

*Why not? I'd gladly let people know what God did in my life, and how He did it. I shared it in my church as a testimony.*

*Wow! Which church do you attend?*

*The Believers Church. That's where I got saved.*

*That's Pastor Joel's church.*

*Yes. And as I said in church this morning, I've come to realise that everyone has a past. The difference is that some are worse than others.*

*You're right.*

Tokunbo's phone began to ring. He didn't recognise the number. Could it be Ruth?

Checking her number on WhatsApp, she found that it was her, and he picked it. "Hello, Ruth,"

"I thought it would be better to call, or are you busy now?"

"No, I'm not. It's okay, you can go on." He said.

"Alright." She said, and began to tell him about her salvation experience and the dreams.

As she talked with him—as if they were old friends—it seemed odd to her because they were not friends at the University.

When she stopped talking, he exclaimed, "Wow! That's so awesome! I'm happy for you. Do you still have such dreams?"

They laughed.

"No, which is a surprise. Well, I had a dream about rapture at a time." She answered.

She told him about the dream, they talked for about five minutes more, and then ended the call.

Three days later, she was in her bedroom folding some clothes while music played on YouTube on her phone. The song playing now was *Look what You've done,* and when it got to the chorus, she sang along, loudly.

*Look what You've done!*
*Look what You've done in me!*
*You spoke Your truth into the lies I let my heart believe,*
*Look at me now!*
*Look how You made me new!*
*The enemy did everything that he could do,*
*Oh, but look what You've done.*

Her phone buzzed and a WhatsApp chat came in. She stopped what she was doing and checked the phone.

The chat was from Tokunbo.

*Hello.*

Ruth responded.

*Hello.*

She put the phone down, took a dress and began to fold it. Her phone sounded again, but she finished folding the dress and put it in her closet before she checked the phone. It was from Tokunbo. He wanted to know if he could call her and she said yes.

He called her almost immediately and after exchanging pleasantries, he asked if she could give her salvation testimony in his church.

"It's very powerful. It will encourage the people especially those who are trusting God for the salvation of their loved ones."

"Which church do you attend?"

"*Christ the Lord Chapel.*"

She hadn't heard the name of the church before, and she asked, "Is it a Pentecostal church?"

"Yes." He answered and told her the name of his pastor.

She considered the invitation briefly and then accepted it. "When would you want me to come?"

"Any Sunday in November would be fine. Let me know the Sunday that's convenient for you, so that I can inform my pastor."

"Okay, I'll let you know by tomorrow. You'll need to send the church's address to me. What time does your service start?"

"Ten in the morning."

"Okay. About how many minutes will I have for my testimony, and am I coming up when some others are giving testimonies?"

"I'll discuss with my pastor and give you the details soon."

"Alright." She said. "So, what do you do in the church?"

He told her that he was the head of the Welfare Department.

Before the call ended, he thanked her again for accepting to come to his church.

Shortly after, she received the address.

The following day, Thursday, she called him.

"I was just going to send a message to you." He said.

They greeted and then he told her that she would have up to thirty minutes for her testimony, and she would come up after other testimonies.

"Ok. I think I'll come on the upper Sunday—November 8." She told him.

"November 8 ... that's the second Sunday of the month," he said thoughtfully. "I think it's okay. I'll let my pastor know. Er... you already have the church's address, right?"

"Yes, I do."

"Okay. The Guest House has two gates. When you get to the street, go past the first gate. At the second gate, you'll see the church's signboard and some ushers. Let the ushers know that I invited you, and they will bring you in."

"Alright, I'll see you then." She said. "I hope I'll recognise you,"

They laughed.

"Why not? I don't think I've changed much. Well, except that I now wear glasses and er ... what else?" He paused briefly and then added, "I have a short beard."

She chuckled.

"Do you still wear glasses?" He wanted to know.

"Yes."

She had a wedding job on Saturday and afterward, she went to church for the Singles Convention. The praise session had begun. Rachel had reserved a seat for her and Ruth went over to meet her. At the appropriate time, Ruth was called and she gave her salvation testimony. She enjoyed every minute of the three-hour service and afterward, she dropped off Rachel at home.

Sunday was the first day of November, and when Ruth returned home from church, she decided to post something on social media. She began to think of the right words to use. Then she remembered one of the two songs that the choir sang in church in the morning—Mercy rewrote my life. She liked the song and when she said so to Rachel after service, Rachel commented that she didn't know who the original artist was, but she knew that Jimmy Swaggart also sang it.

Ruth designed a frame and with the lyrics of the song still in her mind, she typed a text:

*MERCY REWROTE MY LIFE.*

On Instagram, she attached the frame, and in the caption, she wrote:

*Yes, for years, I traveled a road all wrong ...*
*Then, Grace, it placed me right where I belonged*
*When Mercy rewrote my life.*
*Happy Sunday and New Month.*

She looked at the frame and the caption, liked everything, and with a click, she had posted it. She shared the post on Facebook, Twitter, and her WhatsApp status as well.

Saturday, November 7, was her birthday but she had a job and couldn't do anything special to celebrate. It was when she returned home around six-thirty in the evening that she began to return calls and respond to people's congratulatory messages.

The following day, she headed for Tokunbo's church. When she got close, she called his phone, but it was not answered. She located the street, drove to the second gate

of the Guest House, and saw the name of the church by it—
*Christ the Lord Chapel.* Some security men were at the
gate and access was controlled. Inside the compound, she
parked her car and alighted from it.

She told a female usher who approached her that she had
been invited by Tokunbo and as she followed the usher
inside the building, she couldn't help commenting that the
Guest House was beautiful.

When they reached its mirrored reception, she noticed a
framed photograph on the wall, and when she saw the name
on it—Seyi Tomori—she was surprised. Certain that the
man and Tokunbo must be related, she made a mental note
to ask Tokunbo later.

They entered the church hall and just as she was being
shown to a seat, Tokunbo returned her call.

"I'm sorry I missed your call. We were having
departmental prayer. Are you here?"

"Yes, I'm in the church hall."

"Okay, you'll see me soon."

Within two minutes, he and some people emerged from a
room. Coming over, he greeted her and welcomed her to
the church with a broad smile.

"It's good to see you again." He added, and looked
genuinely happy to see her.

"This place is beautiful."

"Thanks, and thanks for coming. Let me introduce you to
my pastor." He said.

He led her to the pastor and his wife, and Ruth greeted them respectfully.

A door near them opened and a man who wore a black suit came out.

"That's my dad. Let me introduce you to him."

"Your dad?" She glanced at the man who she guessed must be in his sixties. He was tall, dark in complexion, and well built.

"Yes."

He took her to his father and as she greeted him, she looked at him closely. Was this not the man in the framed photograph? If yes, did it mean his father owned this place? Really?!

As soon as they left his father, she asked him, "I saw that this place is owned by a Tomori."

He laughed, said yes, and pointed at his father.

"Really? Wow!" Her eyes widened in surprise. "That's nice. What about your mom? Where's she?"

"I think she's praying with someone."

Ruth returned to her seat and he left.

The service started on time and before long, it was time for testimonies. When it was her turn, Ruth got up and went to the front with her bag which contained her camera, phone, and other essentials. She had learned not to leave her bag unattended in a public place, and she knew that thieves could come to even a church.

She sang the song 'You did not wait for me,' and then gave her testimony without giving too much detail.

Immediately the service ended about two hours after, Tokunbo came to her.

"If you're not in a hurry to leave, I can show you around the building. You can also have lunch." He said.

She accepted.

"Please give me some minutes." He said.

While waiting for him, she made a few phone calls.

When he returned, she stood and followed him.

He showed her the big event hall.

"It looks great! I'm surprised that I'm just getting to know about this place." She commented. And then she waved a hand in dismissal and said, "Never mind. I couldn't have known about it with the kind of person I was then."

They laughed.

She spoke again, "I'll definitely tell my clients who are Christians about this place."

"Thanks."

"I have my camera here ... would you mind if I take some pictures to share with people?"

"Oh, no, go ahead."

Bringing out her camera, she set it, and as she began to snap, he watched her.

"I'll send the pictures to some people." She said from behind the camera.

He appreciated her.

"I'll send them to you too."

When she was through, he showed her the lounge, and then she asked, "Can I see the inside of one of the rooms?"

"Sure. Come."

On their way to the reception, they saw a couple coming in their direction, pulling their rolling suitcases, and Tokunbo greeted them familiarly.

At the reception, he asked one of the attendants to open a room so Ruth could see the inside.

"Yes, sir." The attendant said, and taking a hotel key card, he asked them to follow him.

Leading them to a door, he inserted the key card into a card reader which unlocked the door, and they entered the room.

"Wow! This is nice." Ruth said as she looked around the room with a large mirror and floor-to-ceiling closet. From the room's beige curtains to the floor, the furnishings and their arrangement, everything was beautiful. She was impressed. In fact, she had been impressed since she drove inside the compound of the Guest House.

They left the room and the staff member locked the door.

Then Tokunbo led her to the restaurant. Some guests of the House were there, eating. As they entered the large room, heads turned to look at them.

One of the uniformed waiters briskly walked over and greeted them.

"Ade, how are you?" Tokunbo responded.

"I'm fine, sir."

Ruth could hear some music playing in the background as she followed Tokunbo. She knew it would be a Christian song and as she listened, she heard the words 'Thank You, Jesus'. *I guessed as much,* she thought and smiled. She would definitely find time to come back to this place.

Tokunbo greeted some of the guests as he walked her to a table near a window which had a good view of the compound. Ruth could see some people coming inside the compound.

Sitting on a comfortable black chair, she looked at their table, which was covered with gold satin—a tall beautiful vase with artificial flowers stood in the middle of it. The restaurant was lovely.

The waiter produced two laminated menus which he gave them, and they placed their order.

While Tokunbo gave some instructions to the young man, Ruth glanced around the room, admiring the interior décor.

Soon, they were served lemonade, which Tokunbo blessed and as they began to drink it, they continued talking.

She asked, "So, where do you work?"

"Here."

"Why am I not surprised?"

They laughed.

"That's so cool."

He told her how it happened.

The waiter walked up just then, set down their appetizer, and left. Ruth prayed over the appetizer and every other thing that they would eat, and then they continued talking as they picked up their cutleries.

"So, how does it feel to work for your dad?"

He laughed, and then shrugged. "It's okay. We don't have problems."

"Wow! That's great!" She commented. "Some people would never do it. They think it would lead to a major conflict."

He shrugged again. "Well, we're both Christians, and that makes a major difference."

She nodded. "You're right. That's so important."

"I may not agree with him about some things, but why should that lead to conflicts? He's my father so I must respect him. Besides, there's no doubt that a man who built his business to this level has sense."

She nodded again. "Definitely."

"The salary is not bad anyway, so, I can't complain."

They laughed.

It occurred to him to reveal that he was a director in the business and his father was grooming him to take over the business, but he thought it was unnecessary. What did it matter? Besides, how well did he know Ruth? Why should he reveal such a sensitive information to someone who was more or less a stranger?

She spoke again, "When did you become a Christian?"

"I became born again some months after University, during NYSC."

Just then, the waiter returned and removing their used plates, he served the main meals.

# CHAPTER 9

As soon as the waiter left, Ruth said, "You had a drinking problem in school. What caused it?"

He smiled. "Yes. I started drinking at the age of fourteen ... not a lot though."

"Fourteen?!"

"Yes. I had an older brother who also drank alcohol, and I guess it was because we grew up seeing our dad drink almost every evening."

"Oh,"

"At that time, drinking alcohol seemed like fun to me. Then one day, my brother went to a party in my dad's car, got drunk, and had a fatal accident on his way back home."

"Wha-t?!" She exclaimed.

He nodded and looked down into his plate of food with his fork still in his hand, while Ruth dropped her cutlery and looked at him.

He went on. "His death shocked me. I missed him. Not knowing what to do, I turned to alcohol to help me cope. Somehow, it made me feel better, and I gradually began to drink more."

"Oh,"

"My parents were not Christians at the time. My mom blamed my dad for my brother's death. Things were no longer the same at home and my drinking habit became worse. I drank immediately I woke up, and I drank daily."

"Oh, Lord, have mercy!" Ruth exclaimed.

"That plunged me into a downward spiral of bad choices. Of course, I got involved with women, seeking love and happiness, and two of them each had a child for me."

She laughed. "Really?"

He smiled in a sad way and nodded. "It wasn't what I wanted for myself, and I wasn't proud of my actions."

"So, you have two children?"

"Yes, I do. It is what it is." He shrugged and continued. "But nothing I did filled the void in my heart. Very miserable and ashamed of myself, I tried to change my life, to stop drinking, but I always went back to the habit. My promises were always short lived. I was definitely addicted. I told myself that I'd have only a bottle, but found that I couldn't stop. At a time, I thought that it was my lot in life and counselled myself to accept the situation."

*He has gone through a lot,* she thought as she listened to him with rapt attention.

"After the University graduation and I went for the one-year national service, some people in my neighborhood began to invite me to their fellowship, but I always brushed them off. One day, a ten-year-old boy visited my roommate and while they were talking, I heard him ask my roommate if he was going to be an alcoholic because his father was one. That question and the fear on his face really shook me. I thought about my sons ... I definitely wouldn't want them to be like me. I decided to try again, to climb out of the hole that I had dug for myself. This time, I decided to try another way. I went to those neighbors and followed them to church. I confessed that I was addicted and needed help. They ministered to me, I gave my life to Jesus, and the rest—as they say—is history."

"Wow!" Ruth exclaimed again, not sure of what exactly to say.

"With utter reliance on the help of the Holy Spirit, I've been able to turn my life around." He added.

"That's what I hope to achieve too." She said.

"Just continue to follow the leading of the Holy Spirit and you'll be fine." He counseled her. "Are you baptised in the Holy Spirit?"

She nodded and said yes.

"You're on the right path." He assured her.

"Thanks. So, do your children live with you?" She asked.

"Yes."

"Were they in church?"

"Yes, but in the children's department."

They continued talking and when they finished eating, the waiter served them cupcakes for dessert.

"Hmm, delicious! I like this." Ruth said when she had her first bite of a cupcake.

He grinned and nodded.

When they finished eating, she took her camera, got up, and took some pictures of him and the restaurant. She returned to her seat.

He asked, "What made you go into photography in school? How did you start? Have you always liked it?"

She shook her head. "No. I had no interest, it never crossed my mind, but when I needed to do something to make money, someone suggested it. I initially dismissed it, but later considered it and raised money for a camera and training."

"Wow!"

She smiled.

"But that couldn't have been easy."

"No, it wasn't." She admitted. "When I just started, I took pictures of my friends and nature, a lot. They were not so good; most of them were dark and blurry. But I got better with time."

"That's amazing! What you have achieved is awesome. I'm sure you're proud of yourself."

"Thank you."

They continued talking and when she was eventually ready to leave, he saw her off to her car.

"Thanks for coming." He told her and waved. "Drive safely."

"I will, thanks. Bye." She said and waved at him with a smile.

And she was still smiling as she drove out of the compound and down the street. She had enjoyed every minute of the time. Tokunbo was an entirely different person from the person he was back in school. This Tokunbo exuded confidence and godliness, no doubt.

On Tuesday afternoon, she sent all the pictures she took at the Guest House to him, and he called to thank her and let her know that he liked them.

He called her again in the evening. "I sent them to my dad and he likes them. We'd like for you to take some pictures at the Guest House."

She was pleased.

He wanted to know when she'd be available to come over and they fixed the last Wednesday of November.

"Hope I can get some cupcakes to eat afterwards." She said jokingly.

He laughed. "Sure."

They talked for a while longer and when they ended the call, she found that they had spent one hour twenty minutes. Smiling, she thought about him for some minutes.

Taking her phone, she sent a friend request to him on Facebook and followed him on Instagram. Within minutes, he had accepted her friend request on Facebook and followed her back on Instagram.

The days sped by quickly and on that Wednesday, as she prepared to leave her house, she received a chat from Tokunbo to let her know that he had to go out but he hoped to be back before she was through. He informed her that the Hotel manager would attend to her.

At the Guest House, Ruth saw the manager, and did her job like the professional that she was.

She was on her way to see the Accountant for payment when Tokunbo called to say that he was back and would be in his office. When she was leaving the Accountant's office, she asked the man about how to get to Tokunbo's office and he directed her.

In the lobby, she entered the elevator, pressed '3', and it took her to the third floor where she got down.

In Tokunbo's office, they exchanged greetings and she sat down. He wanted to know how things went and she explained all that happened.

He promised to tell some of their guests about her so that they could patronize her and she expressed her appreciation to him.

He called the restaurant on the intercom and asked that lunch for two should be brought to his office. Before long, two waiters brought their food, drinks, and necessary items. He told the waiters that he'd want twelve cupcakes for his visitor to take away, and that the cost should be charged to his account.

When they left, Ruth blessed the delicious food that was set on the table before them, and they began to eat.

They were still eating and talking when the door was knocked and someone entered. Ruth turned and saw one of the waiters carrying a clear plastic cupcake box.

"Oh, thank you." Tokunbo told the man as he set the box down on the table.

Ruth looked at the twelve cupcakes in the clear box and saw that they were topped with strawberries. "These look great! Thank you."

The man left and they continued eating.

Tokunbo said that a pastor was in church the day she came to share her story, and that the pastor would like for her to come to his church to do the same.

She hesitated. "I don't know. I'll have to pray about it."

He nodded. "That's the right thing to do. Pray and let me know your decision."

As soon as they finished eating, she thanked him again for the cakes, lunch, and patronage. Getting on her feet, she carried her bag and the cupcake box.

At home, she prayed about going to the pastor's church as she promised to do, but didn't feel a release in her spirit to honor the invitation.

When she still felt the same way the next day, she called Tokunbo and said no. "I don't feel okay about it. I'm grateful to God for transforming me, but I'll only talk about it when necessary. My past is in the past."

"I understand." Tokunbo commented. "I'll explain to the pastor."

On the first day of December, she sent a new month prayer to Tokunbo and when there was no reply, she guessed that he was busy.

Later in the day around five, he called and after the greetings, he invited her to his church's Christmas Carol that would hold on Saturday evening, December 19.

"That is if you can make it," he added, "I know you're usually busy on Saturday."

"Yes, especially in December." She responded. "I have a wedding job on that day."

"I also have a wedding to attend on the day."

"The groom-to-be has engaged my services since April."

"April?!"

"Yes."

They laughed.

"Being the wedding photographer, I have to be there until I'm no longer needed." She said. "You might know him since he was a year ahead of us in University."

"Oh, we might be talking about the same person." Tokunbo said. "Is he Desmond?"

"Yes."

"Desmond's my cousin." He told her.

"Your cousin?" She was surprised. "Wow!"

He chuckled.

"So, you'll be there?" She wanted to know.

He nodded. "Yes, I have to attend. Desmond won't forgive me if I don't." He said. "I'll be attending with my family."

On Desmond's wedding day, Ruth got to his house around eight in the morning, and began to take pictures.

She took more pictures of Desmond as he and his best-man walked toward the front door, to leave the house, and still more shots outside the house by the groom's decorated car.

In church, as the bride walked inside the hall, and as Desmond looked back to see his bride, Ruth snapped away, capturing their looks, smiles, and the bride's tears.

As she took different shots, she wondered if she would ever wear a white dress like this. But she pushed the pain of the thought aside as quickly as it came and concentrated on what she was doing.

While the choir was singing, she glanced around and located Tokunbo where he sat. His parents were on his left side while two boys were on his right side. She guessed that the boys were his sons.

Focusing the camera in their direction, she took some shots of them. And more shots when they came near the new couple. When the service ended, Tokunbo came to where she was to greet her.

"Are you leaving now?" She wanted to know.

"Not yet. I'll wait for the reception."

The reception held in an event hall across the street, and Ruth eventually got home around seven-thirty in the evening.

Tokunbo sent a message to her around nine.

*How did it go? Are you still there or back at home?*

She replied.

*I got home not quite long. It went well, thanks.*

She would have liked to call him but felt too tired to talk. She sent another message instead to let him know that she would call him the next day.

At about four on Sunday afternoon, she called him.

After the pleasantries, she asked, "The two boys beside you in church, are they your sons?"

He laughed and said yes.

"I guessed as much."

They talked a little about the wedding, and then she said she had a question she'd like to ask him.

"I'm all ears."

"I read online that a Christian could be gay, although I doubt it. What do you think?"

"No, that's not true." He said without hesitation. "It's either a person is gay or a Christian. A person can't be a gay Christian just as a person can't be an alcoholic Christian. It's either we are for God or not for God. We can't serve God and mammon, as the Bible says. Several verses in the Bible warn us not to be deceived, which means that a person can be deceived."

He read some scriptures and warned her to be careful of what she read online.

He continued. "Many of those people online give opinions on issues that they know nothing about or don't understand."

"You're right."

He added, "You're supposed to follow your pastor's teaching unless your pastor is not a man of God. If he is, then follow his teaching, believe God's word in the Bible, and be intimate with the Holy Spirit."

He encouraged her with more words. She thanked him, and they ended the call.

Afterward, she went to bed to rest. She woke up around eight in the evening, and after dinner, she began to work on selecting and enhancing the wedding pictures on her laptop. As she looked at them, she smiled. The pictures were very good and the moments were well captured.

Again, she found herself wondering if she would ever get married. When she realized that the thought was not positive, she prayed to cancel her fears and negative thoughts. "I will get married in Jesus' name."

But when? She didn't have an answer to that.

She focused on her laptop and looking at the pictures, she smiled again. She was actually very good. She was gifted.

Hmm. Was there a reason God gave her this ability? She wondered. If yes, was there a way she could serve God with it? Probably by taking pictures to capture important moments in church? Not certain how to go about it, she made a mental note to discuss with Pastor Ida.

But should she charge a fee for her service or render it free? She needed to be sure before she'd approach Pastor Ida, she thought.

She eventually decided that she would do it free. How could she even ask the church where she got saved and where she was being fed the word of God to pay for her service? No, she could not, she thought.

What if church members would like to patronize her? She decided that she would charge them but give them good discount. Pictures after church service or during church thanksgiving would be free, unless some people asked her to print them out.

She had sixteen pictures for Tokunbo and his family and after enhancing them, she forwarded them to Tokunbo. Afterward, she continued working on the main wedding pictures, certain that Desmond and his bride would love the pictures.

In church on Tuesday, she discussed with Pastor Ida and the woman thought that it was a great idea. She explained that Ruth could take pictures of important moments but it should not be done during sermon or a ministration so that the congregation was not distracted.

# CHAPTER 10

The remaining days of the year sped by quickly and soon, a new year rolled in.

On the third Sunday of February, the church had a special event after the morning service. One of the activities was a dance drama by the church's drama department and choir.

As Ruth watched the ministration, she liked the way a particular lady—a chorister—smiled as she danced. The ministration progressed but her eyes were fixed on the lady. Somehow, Ruth liked her, and she thought that the lady was very beautiful.

When the drama ended and the choir members returned to their assigned place, her eyes searched for the lady among the choristers and found her. Shortly after, it was time for choir ministration, and as they got on their feet to minister, Ruth had eyes only for the lady.

On Tuesday, she was late for Bible study and she quietly went to her class. She glanced around and when she saw the lady, she felt excited.

When she realized what was happening in her mind, she felt troubled, afraid, and discouraged. That which she feared had come upon her. How could this happen to her? And what would she do? How would she overcome this and get rid of her feeling for the lady?

She couldn't concentrate in class, and on the way home, she began to ask God for help. She didn't want to fall back into sin.

She eventually decided to discuss with Tokunbo when he called her on Saturday evening.

"After you got saved, were there times that you still craved alcohol? If yes, how did you handle it? Or did the craving disappear immediately?"

He laughed in a knowing way, and then said, "I know someone who said that the craving stopped immediately, but that's not how it happened for me."

He explained that aside from meditating on God's words concerning the challenge, he had to consciously say no to alcohol and yield to the Holy Spirit daily to overcome the addiction.

"Now, I'm able to walk away from alcohol. I don't even miss it." He added.

"Okay." She said thoughtfully.

He spoke again. "Why did you ask? Are you struggling with your past?"

Taking a deep breath, she said, "Not really, but something happened recently that took me by surprise."

"What's that?"

"I just suddenly began to like a lady in my church and ... I'm somehow scared." She confessed.

"Oh, I see,"

"I've changed ... I've been doing well ... but this sudden feeling for the lady makes me feel bad. I know it's wrong and I should not act on my feelings, but I'm not sure how to handle it."

"Realizing that it's wrong and trying to get help shows that you're born again." He started.

"I'm a little scared."

"You don't need to be scared. The fear is from the devil and the purpose is to destabilize and discourage you." He said. "You should rebuke it."

She took a deep breath.

"Have you prayed about it?"

"Yes, I asked God to help me."

"That's okay but not enough. You need to pray and rebuke that evil spirit that's trying to rear its head by making attempts to return." He said and then told her how to pray.

He added, "Temptations will come, but take note: you don't sin until you act on your feeling. And so, do everything possible not to act on it. Put things in place and stay away from her if necessary."

"She's in the choir, I don't have much interaction with her."

"Good. God knew that challenges would come up and that was why He gave us the Holy Spirit, His word, and the pastor. Satan came to tempt Jesus but Jesus did not fall. You have to be determined to stand for God."

"Okay."

He continued. "When the choir is singing, look away from her or whatever. God will do His part, but you need to do your part—choose not to have a romantic relationship with any female."

She said okay, so he could know that she was listening to him.

"Keep resisting the devil, and yield to the Holy Spirit daily. Eventually you will be fine."

He prayed with her and then added, "Here's another thing—when I became a Christian, the person who was following me up held me accountable, to ensure I did the right thing. So, I'll do the same for you. I will ask you what and how you are doing. Is that okay?"

She chuckled and said yes.

After the call, she prayed more, rebuked the devil, and commanded the feeling for the lady to die in Jesus' name.

About two weeks after, she realized that the feeling had gone and she called Tokunbo to inform him.

She thought about him afterward. She was learning a lot from him and learning more about him. She also felt comfortable with him. He was a good friend.

He called her almost every day to know how she was faring and to answer whatever questions she might have. They shared the word of God, and as they discussed various issues, he could tell that her salvation was genuine, and that she was growing spiritually.

He visited her for the first time on the second Sunday of April. He had told her he would visit around five and she made sure that she got home on time.

After serving him fried chicken and juice, she sat across from him.

They were talking and laughing, and then she asked why he was not yet married.

He laughed.

"I'm just wondering why."

He took a deep breath. "Well, I guess it's because I've been busy putting things in place in my life. I was trying to get my relationship with God right. I've made enough mistakes to last a lifetime."

She laughed.

"I wanted to grow spiritually and be a responsible father to my sons. I have two sons to take care of! Two boys who look up to me." He explained.

She nodded in understanding.

"And with a demanding job thrown into the mix, I just didn't have much time to give marriage a very serious thought."

"You didn't have much time to give marriage a very serious thought? Are you kidding me?"

He laughed.

"I'll tell you what I think. I guess it's because you haven't fallen in love with any of the sisters in your church. Because if you had, busy or not, the case would have been different and you'd be married by now."

He laughed again. "Well, I think you're right. I probably would have gotten married if I'd met the right woman."

"So, my next question is why haven't you met the right woman or fallen in love with one of the ladies in your church?"

He laughed. "To be honest, I've been praying about it, but it just hasn't happened."

"Well, that's okay. I'm sure it will happen soon. Take your time." She said. "But I hope your parents don't put pressure on you to get married?"

"They do,"

She laughed. "Parents!"

"Not a lot though." He added.

"Most parents are like that, especially mothers." She commented. "I guess they mean well."

"Yes, they do."

He wanted to ask if she'd started praying about marriage to the right man, but changed his mind. Marriage should not be rushed into.

They continued talking and laughing, and he eventually left around seven-thirty.

Some time later that evening, she allowed herself to think about marriage and her future. She believed that she was ready for marriage and she began to pray that she would meet her husband and fall in love him.

To her surprise, Pastor Joel and his wife visited her on the first day of May. She offered them juice, but they declined and said that they just decided to visit in order to know how she was doing.

"Have you heard from Linda lately?"

"Not really, but someone told me she's married." She answered.

"Married? Really?" The pastors were surprised.

She nodded and smiled.

"Who did she marry? A man or a woman?"

"A man."

"Interesting." Pastor Ida said

They wanted to know how Ruth had been handling her old friends and she said that she had lost most of them.

"They think I've lost my mind." She said and laughed.

She remembered her discussion with one of them recently and decided to mention it. "I tried to preach to one of them last month but she didn't want to listen. She was arguing that monogamous same sex relationship should be acceptable to God, but I said no."

"You're right, it's not acceptable. God's word is clear about it." Pastor Ida responded.

"Same partner doesn't make it right." Pastor Joel added.

By way of encouragement, they mentioned some scriptures that warn against deception and walking in the flesh. Afterward, they prayed for her and left.

When Tokunbo called her on Monday evening, he said he'd be traveling to New York, USA, in July for a three-month course.

He eventually traveled on August 3 and when he got there, he sent a message to her that he arrived safely.

They kept in touch on WhatsApp and as soon as he got a phone number, he gave it to her and they talked regularly.

In the first week of October, he told her that he'd be returning to Nigeria on November 1. He wanted to know what she'd want him to buy for her.

"Anything." She responded and laughed. "I'd appreciate whatever you give me."

"I mean something for your business, perhaps."

"For my business? Really?!" She was surprised. "You wouldn't mind to do that?"

He laughed. "Well, I wouldn't mind if it's something I can afford. The weight is not a problem because I'm getting some things for the Guest House which will be sent by cargo."

Elated, she thanked him profusely, and mentioned a particular equipment.

As she talked, she searched for it online. "It's about sixty nine dollars. I don't know if it's within your budget. If not, I can -"

"It's okay. I can afford that." He said and laughed. "Is that all?"

She said yes, and thanked him again.

After the call, he ordered the equipment online and two days after, it was delivered to him.

He also bought gifts for his family, pastors, some friends, and a jewelry set for Ruth since her birthday would be on November 7.

He returned to Nigeria on Monday, November 1, and on Wednesday evening, he visited her, carrying a big box.

She opened the door and welcomed him with a broad smile.

Placing the box on a table, he sat down.

She served him some refreshments and as he ate, they talked.

Then he opened the big box and brought out the jewellery box.

"This is for your birthday on Sunday." He held it out.

She was greatly surprised. "Oh, thank you."

Collecting it, she opened it and found an elegant jewellery set. She thanked him again.

He brought out the equipment, gave it to her, and she thanked him.

They continued talking and then he asked, "What's your plan for your birthday?"

"Oh, thanks for bringing that up ... I almost forgot." She said. "Two of my friends in church insist on coming over to celebrate with me, so I've told them that we'll go out for dinner. I'll call my siblings this evening or tomorrow morning, and probably my parents, to invite them too. I'm thinking that we should meet at a restaurant around five on Sunday. Please, say you'll come."

"Okay, I'll try to be there." He said and smiled. "Er ... if you're thinking of going to a restaurant, why don't you come to the restaurant at the Guest House? It will be on me, I'll take care of it."

"Really? Is the restaurant open to people who are not guests?"

"No, but you can come as my guests."

"Wow! That would be great!" She exclaimed and thanked him. "There may be about ..." As she mentioned names, she counted on her fingers, "about nine or ten people. Is that okay?"

When he said yes, she took her phone. "I need to send a message to inform them right away. What time should it be? Is five okay?"

"It's fine."

She began to type on her phone. When she finished, she sent the message to the relevant people and then put the phone down.

When he was ready to leave, she got up to see him off.

She told him, "Thanks again for everything—the equipment and the jewelry and the offer to host my birthday celebration—I appreciate it."

"Glad to help."

Rachel called her in the morning of the next day and asked, "What's going on between you and that guy?"

"Which guy?"

"Tokunbo."

Ruth burst into laughter. "Nothing. Why did you ask?"

"You talk about him a lot. I haven't met him, but I know a great deal about him already. And now, he's hosting your birthday!"

"He's hosting my birthday, gave me a jewelry set and photography equipment." Ruth added and laughed again.

"Hold it! I don't understand. Please rewind."

Ruth laughed again and explained, "I told you that he traveled to America. The jewelry and the equipment are what he bought for me."

"Wow! Are you sure there's nothing going on?"

Ruth laughed. "Nothing, we're just friends. He's just being nice."

When she woke up on Sunday morning, she found several messages on her phone, of people wishing her a happy birthday. She responded to a few of them before getting up to prepare for church.

She returned home around one-thirty, and while responding to the congratulatory messages, she received Tokunbo's call. He wanted her to know that he'd be in a meeting soon, but that he'd made necessary arrangements for her. He would join them as soon as he could. He gave her the names of the two waiters who would attend to her and her company.

Realizing that she'd have to get to the venue before the others she'd invited because of this arrangement, Ruth stopped what she was doing. She quickly had a shower, got dressed, and left the house to pick up Rachel and her parents.

They got to the Guest House on time and went to the restaurant which was busy with the hum of people who were eating and having a nice time. Ruth asked for one of the two assigned waiters, and the man took them to a table.

When the others arrived, the waiter gave them the menu, and they ordered a three-course meal.

Ruth and her company had had the appetizer—Ruth's was peppered gizzard—and the waiters were clearing the table to serve the main meal when Tokunbo appeared. He greeted everyone warmly, went to Ruth, and as he wished her a happy birthday with a brief hug, he noticed that she wore the jewelry he gave her. Afterward, he sat with them.

They spent about three hours in the restaurant and enjoyed every minute. They prayed, sang, someone gave a brief word of exhortation, and the three-course meal they had was delicious. Tokunbo had to handle Ruth's camera and he did a good job of capturing the moment which made her see another side of him.

He smiled a lot and she realized that she liked his smile. *He has a very nice smile.*

They eventually left and when he was seeing them off, Ruth's parents thanked him for hosting their daughter's birthday.

Her mother added, "Extend my greetings to your wife and children."

Ruth burst into laughter.

"Why are you laughing? He's not married?"

"No, Mom." Ruth said. "Why would you even assume that he's married?"

Everyone laughed.

"Well, you should say a big Amen, Tokunbo!" Rachel commented.

Smiling, Tokunbo did.

When Ruth eventually returned to her house, she called Tokunbo to appreciate him again.

"Well, did you enjoy yourself?"

"Yes, I did. I had a wonderful time."

They talked for some minutes. When they were about to end the call, she teased him, "Extend my greetings to your wife and children."

They laughed.

"Extend my greetings to your husband." He teased her back.

"You didn't add my children." She pointed out.

"Yes, and your children."

"I will, thank you." She said, still laughing.

When their laughter subsided, he wanted to know if she had started praying about marriage, and she said yes.

"Definitely. I'm ready for my husband." She said confidently.

"Great. Good to hear that. Awesome!"

She explained, "The way I see it is this ... I don't have to love every man. What I need and which I'm praying for is to meet my husband, fall in love with him, and move forward."

Later in bed, she checked the pictures that Tokunbo snapped at the restaurant and found that they were good.

Afterward, she allowed herself to think about him.

And then, she considered how he'd been nice to her and the attention he gave her at the restaurant. Did he like her as a woman or was he just being nice as a friend?

She wasn't sure what it might be, but she knew that she liked everything about him. He was reliable. And he was the kind of man she could risk giving her heart to—the kind that could handle her. Also, she liked his smile and laugh— a lot.

Another thing she liked about him—he knew everything about her and she didn't have to pretend or be careful around him. She could discuss anything with him.

She began to pray that God would give her a man like Tokunbo, make her recognize him, and fall in love with him as he would with her.

As she prayed, she thought of other things she liked about him—he was handsome and very nice. And she was still thinking about how handsome and nice he was when she eventually fell asleep around midnight.

Tokunbo's father and mother were going to celebrate their birthday—sixty five and sixty respectively—on Saturday, December 18, and Ruth was booked as the photographer.

She was happy to be hired by them, and she prayed that more of such people with influence and wealth would hire her. However, working for such people also put her under great pressure because she knew that one good word from them could make her and one bad word from them could break her.

As she thought about being made or broken by these people, she could hear the Holy Spirit telling her that if she allowed God to be in control of her life, no one would be able to break or destroy what she had labored for, and she would not be at the mercy of the devil.

She quickly changed her opinion and prayed that God would lead and prosper her.

She suggested a photoshoot before the event which Tokunbo and his parents thought would be nice, and a day was fixed.

On the day, she went to their house with a Christmas gift for Tokunbo and birthday gifts for his parents.

Tokunbo received them and then led her to the living room so she could set up her equipment. Glancing around, she liked everything she saw—beautiful paintings and enlarged family pictures adorned the beige wall of the exquisitely furnished large living room.

A lady came in and Tokunbo introduced her as his sister.

Soon his parents were ready and as Ruth got to work, they liked her professionalism.

On the day of the celebration, she got to the reception hall at the Guest House earlier than the guests, so she could take pictures of the guests as they arrived. She made sure that the memorable event was well covered by taking several pictures of the celebrants and their immediate family members.

She was able to talk with Tokunbo's sons, and when she was on phone with Tokunbo later, she told him that they were well behaved.

The more she saw and talked with Tokunbo, the more she thought about him and liked him.

On New Year's Day, Saturday, when she realized that he was the first person she called to wish a Happy New Year, she knew that she thought of him and liked him a lot. Some things about him tugged at her heart in ways she hadn't expected.

And when she was still thinking of him on Friday evening, a week later, she wondered what was happening. She had prayed to have a man like him, not him in particular! So where was this feeling coming from? Tokunbo could not marry someone like her, could he? Why would he?

She turned in bed and took a deep breath. How should she handle this? She usually discussed things with Tokunbo, and she would have loved to discuss this matter with him, but it was about him and she knew that she should not.

Turning to God, she asked, "Is this love?" This was somehow different from what she felt for the women. This felt right.

*And if it is love, how can I fall in love with Tokunbo, of all men?! He's not likely to return the feeling! How did this happen*? She wondered, troubled.

*Help me, Lord*!

But her attraction to him kept growing, and when January ended with Tokunbo still on her mind, she wondered why God seemed not to realise that she had a challenge. And this was a time she would appreciate a dream from God to direct her, but there was none, and she had to rely solely on God's words and her knowledge of Him.

Tokunbo invited her to a seminar that would hold in his church on February 23, and she decided to attend. She got there a little early, saw his parents, and went over to greet them. His sons were also there and she chatted with them a little.

On the way home around ten in the evening, she was thinking about the odds against marriage to Tokunbo. Marriage to him came with two sons. She loved children, and had already begun to love his sons, but would she make a good stepmother? And would the two boys accept her?

Another concern was cooking. She didn't cook much, but as a married woman, she would have to cook and feed her family. She thought about this and told herself that cooking should not be a problem. She could learn how to cook some meals.

His parents were another concern. Would they want her? She wasn't sure and she took a deep breath.

The Scripture *for with God nothing will be impossible,* came to her mind and in her room at home, she went on her knees and prayed for God's grace and help. She might not know what God had in store for her, but she knew He was with her still.

She also knew that she should not allow her past to deflate her self-worth.

# CHAPTER 11

Tokunbo was surprised that he was thinking of Ruth a great deal. When he realized that it might be love, he began to pray, asking God to take control and lead him. He couldn't afford to make a mistake.

He had feelings for her and she was a Christian, no doubt, but why should he marry her? Was she the right one for him?

And what would people say, considering her past? He chewed over this particular question thoroughly and reasoned that—yes, people's opinion mattered but God's opinion mattered more.

So, what was God's opinion about marriage to her? He considered this and concluded that he could marry her since she had become a committed child of God. He should focus on her present and future. Her past should not matter.

As he reflected on this, he wondered, "What do I love about her?"

He thought about the question and told himself that he liked the fact that she had strength, courage, and confidence. She was also focused, hardworking, honest, and open.

And the way she had allowed God to transform her life didn't cease to amaze him. Hmm.

As he searched his heart for more reasons to choose her, more questions occurred to him. *Can she love me? Does she have feelings for me? Are we even compatible?*

While he was pondering these in his heart, another question rose up. *Will she be able to have children? Will she even want to have children?*

He realized he would need to pray more and to also ask Ruth some relevant questions that would give him answers.

He contacted her and when she said that she'd be at home on Wednesday, March 9, he visited her in the afternoon.

She offered him food, but he declined and accepted to drink juice.

As they talked and laughed, he thought of a way to navigate the discussion to what he had in mind. When she said something about her past life, he seized the opportunity.

"At that time, did it occur to you at anytime to remove your womb?" He asked her.

She smiled and shook her head. "No, I loved children and wanted one or two. The plan at that time was for Linda to conceive by some means, but if it wasn't possible for some reasons, I would get pregnant. I love children, they are beautiful."

He nodded. Some of his questions had been answered. "About how many children would you like to have when you get married?"

Still smiling, she answered, "I'd like to have three or four."

"Four? Wow!" He exclaimed.

They laughed.

"It will have to be with my husband's agreement of course." She added.

He asked some questions about her past and Linda, questions that would make him see into her heart and as she answered, he listened carefully.

When there was no further question from him, she decided to ask him about his past too. She wanted to know where his baby mamas were, how involved they were in his sons' lives, and if he sometimes talked to them. He answered her.

Over the next few days, the more he interacted with her, the more his feelings grew, and the more he prayed. He also discussed with his sister and one of his friends.

When he became sure of his love for her and God's involvement, he decided to talk to her. He called to know when she'd be available so he could visit her, and they fixed Monday, March 21.

She didn't know why he wanted to see her but she looked forward to his visit.

That day, he arrived around six-thirty in the evening and as she served him soft drink and exchanged pleasantries with him, he looked at her. Yes, he loved her, he was sure.

Then she told him, "You said you'd like to see me."

"Yes." Putting down the glass cup he was holding, he sat forward and said, "I've been praying ... about you, Ruth." He paused.

She frowned. *Praying about me? Why*? She sat up and focused on him. He was looking steadily at her.

"I love you."

The frown suddenly disappeared as her eyes widened and her mouth turned at the sides in a smile for some seconds in speechless disbelief. Her right hand went up to cover her mouth in shock.

He took a deep breath, not very certain of what she would say.

He reached out, pulled her hand from her mouth and held it as he spoke again, "I want you to pray about us, me. I'd like to marry you."

"Oh my God!" She exclaimed and put her other hand on her heart. "Oh my God! I've also been praying, Tokunbo! I love you!" She said enthusiastically.

Elated, he began to talk about the exact moment he realized that she was the one for him and of all the things that he loved about her.

"I know you're the one I'd like to spend the rest of my life with." He added.

Smiling broadly, she revealed how she had been feeling about him for some time, and then she asked him the one question that had been plaguing her mind, "What about your parents? Have you told them?"

"No."

Sensing that his parents might not easily agree, they decided to pray for divine intervention for about a week, after which he would inform them.

They also talked about various issues ranging from their careers, and his sons, to their spiritual lives.

In the evening of Saturday, April 2, Tokunbo informed his parents and he saw their smiles turn to frowns.

"That lady?! Ruth?!" His mother wasn't sure she'd heard him right.

He nodded.

"Why?!" His father asked, obviously concerned. "She may be a Christian, but why should she be the one you've chosen to marry?"

This was one of the questions he had asked himself and he gave his parents his answer.

But his father didn't agree with him. He added, "Someone told me about a woman who left her husband after a child, to be fully gay."

"I'm sure that the woman was not a Christian," Tokunbo responded easily.

"The person who told me said that she was a Christian,"

"Daddy, I'm sure you know who a Christian is. Such a thing won't happen if a person is truly a Christian and is following the leading of the Holy Spirit. I believe that Ruth's truly saved."

They continued talking, and still concerned, they asked if he had mentioned it to his sister, and he said yes.

"And what did she say?"

"Well, she asked me to pray about it and inform you."

"What about the parish pastor?"

He shook his head. "I haven't. I wanted to mention it to you first."

"Well, I'd advise you pray more," his father said. "I don't think this is a wise choice."

His mother came to his room later and began to talk to him. "We want the best for you, and we want you to have a good marriage."

"I know, Mom, and I'm careful."

"Being a Christian—truly saved—is one thing, and being able to have a good marriage is another thing. Besides, how can you know what she has done to her body?"

"What do you mean?"

"Will she be able to have children?" She asked. "What if her womb has been removed?

"Her womb has not been removed."

"How would you know?"

"We discussed it." He answered.

She asked him some questions and then advised him to pray more and see their pastor. "I've been praying for you and I will pray about this."

In bed at night, he called Ruth to let her know he had discussed with his parents and would be seeing his parish pastor the next day. After the call, he began to reflect on his parents' concerns and reasoning about his decision, to determine if God was trying to tell him something. As he gave it a serious thought, he also prayed and asked God to take control.

After church service the next day, he went to the pastor.

When he stopped talking, the pastor was silent for about a minute as he considered what Tokunbo had just told him. Then he said, "I'd like to talk to her and ask her some questions. Let her come to church on Sunday, and I'll talk to her after the service."

Ruth came to the church the next Sunday, April 10, and when the service ended, Tokunbo took her to the pastor. The pastor called his wife and the four of them sat in the pastor's meeting room.

As they asked Ruth some questions and considered her answers, they also considered her appearance and demeanour. They did not find her lacking.

The pastor asked another question, "Has salvation cost you anything?"

"Yes, sir."

She said that some of the things she'd lost were her pride and some friends, and she went on to explain how she lost the friends.

"I'd known some of them for long and we were very close. It really bothered me when some of them began to treat me like an enemy. It was painful, but I knew that I was on the right path and I had to let them go."

"All of them?"

"Some of them didn't care what I did but when I tried to share the word of God with them, they disappeared. I've been praying for them though."

As they talked, Tokunbo looked at them and listened.

"What about the lady, Linda?" The pastor's wife asked.

"I don't see her. I ran into her only once since she left my apartment -"

"Did you talk when you ran into her?"

She shook her head. "Not much. But I don't miss the life, and by God's grace, I've never looked back."

"What can you say helped you to stay away?"

"I'd say it's because I was genuinely converted and properly discipled." Ruth answered.

She added, "My encounter with God—knowing that God loves me—has also helped to keep me standing."

"Okay."

She added, "Besides, I learned that she's married now."

The pastor and his wife expressed surprise.

They also asked Tokunbo some questions and afterward, Ruth and Tokunbo left. In the evening, the pastor and his wife called Tokunbo and his parents, and told them that they thought Ruth was genuinely born again, but that Tokunbo would need to see the senior pastor.

A day was fixed and, on the day, April 20, Tokunbo took Ruth to the senior pastor at the church headquarters. He talked with them, asked both of them series of questions, and asked them to see him again on Monday, to allow him pray.

That day, April 25, the senior pastor asked further questions, counseled them, and eventually gave his approval.

Tokunbo's parents had also been praying and observing Ruth whenever she visited him in their house or at work. And on the last day of April, they told Tokunbo that if she was his choice, they would support him.

They asked him to bring her and when she came, they counseled and prayed for them.

Afterward, Ruth and Tokunbo arranged for their families to meet.

They also met with Ruth's pastors—Pastors Joel and Ida—who said they would need to go through premarital counseling and as soon as the wedding date was fixed, Ruth should get the church administrator informed.

"Also, a week to the wedding day, Ruth will need to go for pregnancy test. I trust my spiritual children, but this is a practice in this church to be sure that both of you have honored God in your relationship." Pastor Joel added.

Over the next few weeks, Tokunbo and Ruth got to know more about each other as they called each other daily and visited when they could. She also attended some of his church events, and he came to hers.

They began to discuss and plan their wedding and future. Their wedding was scheduled for the third Saturday of December while the traditional wedding ceremony would hold a day before at an event hall not too far from her parents' house. The church wedding would hold in her church while the reception would be at the big event hall of the Guest House.

"Since you're the one getting married, who will be the wedding photographer?" Tokunbo asked her, and they laughed.

"That's not a problem at all. It will be taken care of." She said. "I've informed two of my colleagues already."

Rachel, who was the maid of honor, made the beaded jewelry that Ruth wore for the traditional wedding.

On the wedding day, one of the two photographers came to Ruth's parents' house while the other was with Tokunbo.

At the right time, Ruth left the house and went to church in a well-decorated car.

Soon, it was time to enter the church and she made her way to the entrance of the hall, looking very beautiful in her white wedding gown. Cameras and phones clicked away.

She held her flowers in her left hand, and linked her right arm with her father's left arm. Stepping inside the hall, they walked down the aisle as the congregation sang the hymn—All hail the power of Jesus name—which she chose. Rachel was behind her, carrying out her duty as the best lady.

The service progressed, and soon they were asked to face each other, hold hands, and exchange their marital vows. With a glowing face, she looked at Tokunbo and smiled. Tokunbo, who wore a well-tailored navy-blue suit, returned the smile with joy.

The service started at ten in the morning and ended at twelve-twenty in the afternoon. Outside the hall, the new couple took pictures with families and friends before heading to the reception hall at the Guest House.

The event started at one-forty and lasted about three hours.

Afterward, some of their friends hung around for some time, and those who traveled down for the ceremony were lodged in the Guest House till the next day.

Tokunbo and Ruth were finally alone in their suite around eight in the evening. Food was brought to their room and after eating, Ruth had a shower, wore the nightdress she had bought for her wedding night, and got in bed.

Tokunbo was on the phone and when he was through, he got in bed beside her, and turned off the bedside lamp. He turned to her and she eagerly went into his arms.

Afterward, still wrapped in each other's arms, he looked at her lovingly and said, "I enjoyed that. What about you? Did you?"

She smiled and nodded, her heart full of so much love and gratitude. "Umm hmm."

"What does that mean?"

"Yes, I did." She answered softly.

She spoke again, "God had a lot of mercy on me when He saved me."

"Yes, and He had a lot of mercy on me too when He saved me." He added.

They didn't talk for some seconds, each lost in thoughts of spending a lifetime loving, learning, and growing together.

Then, pulling her closer, he declared, "I love you."

"I love you."

# ALSO BY TAIWO IREDELE ODUBIYI

## FICTION

**Pratt Sisters Series**
In Love for Us * Tears on My Pillow * To Love Again

**Femi and Ibie Series**
With This Ring * The Forever Kind of Love

**Agape Campus Church Series**
You Found Me * Life Goes On * My Desire

**Bible Stories**
What Changed You? * Too Much of a Good Thing

**The Past Series**
Shadows from the Past * This Time Around * Then Came You

**Baby Miracle Series**
Oh Baby! * Sea of Regrets

**Redirected Series**
Is it Me You're Looking for? * Marriage on Fire * Shipwrecked With You

### Mercy & friends Series

The Forever Kind of Love * If You Could See Me Now * Accidentally Yours

### Stand Alone Titles

Love Fever * Love on the Pulpit * My First Love * The One for Me * When A Man Loves A Woman * I'll Take You There * Never Say Never!

## FOR CHILDREN

Rescued by Victor * No One is a Nobody * Greater Tomorrow * The Boy Who Stole * Joe and His Stepmother, Bibi * Nike & the Stranger * Billy the Bully * Jonah's First Day of School * Bimbo Learns a Lesson

## NONFICTION

30 Things Husbands Do That Hurt Their Wives * 30 Things Wives Do That Hurt Their Husbands * Rape & How to Handle it * Devotionals for Singles * God's Words to Singles * God's Words to Couples * God's Words to Older Adults * Real Answers, Real Quick! (for singles) * Real Answers, Real Quick! (for couples) * Divine Instructions to live by – 1 * Divine Instructions to live by – 2 * God's Words to Women in Ministry

# ABOUT THE AUTHOR

Taiwo Iredele Odubiyi is a Pastor and the Executive President of TenderHearts Family Support Initiative, a Non-Governmental Organization, and Pastor Taiwo Odubiyi Ministries. She has a deep and strong passion for relationships and expresses this in ministries - nationally and internationally- to children, teenagers, singles, women and couples. She reaches out to these groups through counseling, seminars and programs such as Tenderheartslink, an online program for Christian singles and couples. Married and blessed with children, she is the host of the YouTube program - It's all about you! This is the twenty ninth of her soul-lifting and life-changing novels.

*I love hearing from the readers of my books. If this book has blessed you, please send your comments to:*
WhatsApp: +1(443)694-6228
Website: www.pastortaiwoodubiyi.org
Facebook: Pastor Mrs. Taiwo Odubiyi
        Pastor Taiwo Iredele Odubiyi's novels & books
        Tenderheartslink with Pastor Taiwo Odubiyi
Instagram: @pastortaiwoiredeleodubiyi

*If you have friends and loved ones, then you do have people you should bless with copies of these very interesting and life-changing novels and books!*

Made in the USA
Middletown, DE
20 October 2022